PUFFIN B

MORRIS GL

Second Childhood

Morris Gleitzman was born and educated in England. He went to Australia with his family in 1969 and studied for a degree. In 1974 he began work with the ABC, left to become a full-time film and television writer in 1978 and went on to write numerous television scripts. He has two children and lives in Melbourne, but visits England regularly. Now one of the best-selling children's authors in Australia, his first children's book was *The Other Facts of Life*, based on his award-winning screenplay. This was followed by the highly acclaimed *Two Weeks With the Queen*, and he has since written many other books for children including *Second Childhood*, *Totally Wicked!* (with Paul Jennings), and *Bumface*.

MORRIS GLEITZMAN

SECOND CHILDHOOD

PUFFIN BOOKS

For Chris, Sophie and Ben

PUFFIN BOOKS

Published by the Penguin Group
Penguin Books Ltd, 27 Wrights Lane, London W8 5TZ, England
Penguin Putnam Inc., 375 Hudson Street, New York, New York 10014, USA
Penguin Books Australia Ltd, Ringwood, Victoria, Australia
Penguin Books Canada Ltd, 10 Alcorn Avenue, Toronto, Ontario,
Canada M4V 3B2
Penguin Books (NZ) Ltd, Private Bag 102902, NSMC, Auckland, New Zealand

On the World Wide Web at: www.penguin.com

Penguin Books Ltd, Registered Offices: Harmondsworth, Middlesex, England

First published in Australia by Penguin Books Australia Ltd 1990
Published in Puffin Books 1995
5 7 9 10 8 6

Made and printed in England by Clays Ltd, St Ives plc

British Library Cataloguing in Publication Data
A CIP catalogue record for this book is available from the British Library

ISBN 0–140–36878–7

All around the hall, people were turning to look at him, smiling and clapping.

Teachers.

Parents.

Kids.

Mum and Dad were beaming at him and hugging him and saying things he couldn't hear because the applause was so loud.

Dad's eyes were shining.

Mum's cheeks were wet.

Then he was on his feet, squeezing past lots of knees, walking towards the stage where Mrs Bryant stood waiting. She was beaming at him too, looking more like an Aunty than the headmistress who had once yelled at him for washing a live frog in the bubbler.

He climbed the wooden steps onto the stage and Mrs Bryant held up her hands. The clapping stopped. Mrs Bryant put her hand on his shoulder.

'Mark Smalley,' she said in a loud voice, 'congratulations on being this year's outstanding pupil, the Dux of the School.'

She shook his hand and gave him a small box covered in velvet.

'We hope,' she went on, 'that this prize will inspire you to even greater achievements next year in high school.'

The applause started again, louder than ever.

He stood on the stage and gazed out over the rows of faces. He saw Mum and Dad looking up at him, glowing with pride and pleasure.

Mark let the applause pour into him and fill him up until his head overflowed with the things he was going to do.

First, he thought, I'll discover a cure for all the kids who have to wear metal things on their legs.

Then I'll design a Porsche that mums and dads can afford.

Then I'll invent a cake recipe that makes people live an extra hundred years. Two hundred if they have another slice . . .

'Smalley . . .'

Mark gave a start.

A voice, almost drowned out by the applause.

'Smalley . . .'

But getting louder.

'Smalley . . .'

And angrier.

'Smalley . . .'

For a moment Mark didn't know where he was.

Then Mr Cruickshank's agitated face appeared centimetres from his and Mr Cruickshank's bony knuckles tapped him on the head.

'Planet Earth calling Mark Smalley,' said Mr Cruickshank. 'Anyone in there?'

Mark remembered exactly where he was.

High school.

Thursday arvo.

History class.

He heard giggles from around the classroom.

'Welcome back,' said Mr Cruickshank. 'Now if you've finished daydreaming, perhaps you could answer my question.'

Mark felt panic bubbling up inside him.

What question?

He looked desperately past Mr Cruickshank, searching for a clue.

He saw Pino Abrozetti, who was standing out the front for talking, put his finger on his nose.

Was that a clue?

Mark wasted vital seconds wondering why a history teacher would ask a question about noses before he realized Pino wasn't pointing to his nose, he was picking it.

Then Mark saw the live sheep tethered to the leg of Mr Cruickshank's desk. A living resource, Mr Cruickshank had called it earlier. And chalked on the blackboard were the words 'Australian Wool Exports 1850–1890'.

Mark knew he'd have to have a bash.

'Um . . .' he said, 'sheep?'

The class broke into titters and a forest of hands flew up.

Mr Cruickshank, whose nose was starting to go pink, waved the hands down with a pile of essays and gave a big sigh.

'If you don't wake up to yourself, Smalley,' he said, 'do you know what you're going to end up as?'

Is he repeating the first question, wondered Mark, or asking a new one?

He looked down. And before he could stop himself, he was beckoning Mr Cruickshank closer.

Mr Cruickshank bent down again, puzzled.

'I said,' he repeated, 'do you know what you're going to end up as?'

'Sheep's poop, sir,' whispered Mark.

Mr Cruickshank looked startled.

'I wouldn't have put it quite like that,' he said.

'You've trodden in some, sir,' said Mark as quietly as he could. A person who's trodden in sheep's poop doesn't want the whole world to know.

The class exploded into barely suppressed laughter.

Mr Cruickshank glared at Mark, at the class, at his shoe, and at the trail of messy footprints between his feet and the sheep.

'I don't know why I bother,' said Mr Cruickshank bitterly to the sheep.

He turned back to Mark.

'The past doesn't mean a thing to you, does it, Smalley?'

Mark thought about explaining that it did mean a thing to him, a lot of things, and that he'd rather be there now.

He decided not to.

Mr Cruickshank gave another sigh and dropped a project onto Mark's desk.

Mark closed his eyes. This was the moment he'd been dreading. Please, he thought, don't let me get worse than a C.

He opened his eyes and stared at the letter in red ink on the first page of the project.

D.

Mark felt a cold sinking feeling in his stomach.

Mr Cruickshank was crouching down again, face close to his.

'Not good enough, Smalley,' he said. 'Everyone here did well in primary school. That's history. This is high school. Wake up to yourself, Smalley.'

Mark looked at the sheep.

The sheep looked dolefully back at him.

'Baaaa,' said the sheep.

That's right, thought Mark. A bloke can't come top all the time.

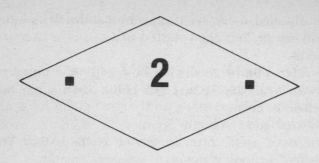

2

M ark cleared his throat and read from the piece of paper in his hand.

'Mum, Dad, it's like this. High school isn't as easy as primary school. It's much harder to get A's all the time in high school. Take me for example. No matter how hard I try I can't get better than B minus. I've even had a couple of C's. I think there might have been a D at some stage as well.'

'That's great,' said Rufus.

The bus lurched to a halt. Pino clambered out of the seat behind them and looked over Mark's shoulder.

'Lousy handwriting,' he yelled back at them as he jumped off the bus. 'B minus.'

'Can I copy that?' asked Rufus, rummaging in his bag and pulling out a leaky pen and an exercise book with a sandwich stuck to it. 'I'd like to say that to my mum.'

'You can have it,' said Mark, giving him the piece of paper. 'I've learnt it off by heart.'

'I'll have to change the last bit,' said Rufus. As the

bus pulled away he threw the sandwich out the window at Pino, then started writing in the exercise book.

After a bit he read what he'd written. 'No matter how hard I try I can't get better than D's. Mark Smalley reckons that's pretty good going for a kid whose dad's left home.'

'Good,' said Mark. 'Are you going to tell her today?'

'I'll wait till you've told yours,' said Rufus. 'See if they hit you.'

Mark stopped at the front gate, took a deep breath, then stepped into the front yard.

Joy Smalley was on her knees, watering a row of young trees that were barely higher than the fence.

'Mum,' said Mark, 'it's like this.'

Joy carried on watering.

Mark realized she couldn't hear him because of the traffic roaring past.

He shouted. 'Mum, it's like this.'

She still didn't look up.

Mark went over and stood right behind her and yelled.

'Mum, it's like this.'

She looked up, saw it was him, and grinned.

'Hi love,' she shouted. 'I've got them.' She pointed to the saplings. 'I decided to go with the four rather than save up for the six.'

'Mum,' shouted Mark, 'it's . . .'

But Joy had turned back to the trees. 'Man at the nursery reckons they're the toughest breed of tree on the market,' she yelled.

'Mum . . .'

'Cross between an ironbark and a something else. Any rate, tougher than that wimpy grass seed.' She pulled a few wispy strands of brown grass out of the dirt.

'Mum . . .'

'Man at the nursery reckons he's seen this breed of tree grow through concrete.' She flicked a tiny bug off one of the leaves. 'Get off there, you little vandal.'

Mark tapped her on the shoulder. She looked up. Mark pointed to his mouth. She stood up, concerned.

'What is it, love? Do you need to go to the dentist?'

She watched Mark shake his head and trudge wearily into the house. Poor love, she thought, must be tough at the top.

Inside, Mark dumped his school bag, got a drink and a Milo sandwich, and started planning how he was going to break the news about his grades to Dad.

Bob Smalley pulled into the driveway, nearly demolishing a young tree.

He turned off the engine and sat for a moment in the old Falcon, enjoying the peace and quiet.

He knew it wasn't really peace and quiet, but after eight hours of knocking buildings down with a bulldozer, it was close enough.

He looked at the pile of demolition salvage stacked

next to the house, the old doors and window frames and bathroom fittings and pieces of timber, and daydreamed for a bit.

Country cottage in that lot, he thought, if I could afford the bit of country to build it on.

Then he braced himself and got out of the car.

The traffic roar hit him like a punch in the ears.

He went over and checked the bolts in the FOR SALE sign on the front fence. They were holding out pretty well considering how much traffic vibration they'd had to withstand over the last three years.

Bob looked at the six lanes of vehicles thundering past. He looked up at the new flyover, four more lanes of traffic howling past almost directly above his head.

He had a swear at the planners who could turn a bloke's quiet suburban corner into a raving madhouse with a flick of a pen. He thought of popping over to their quiet mansions in one of the boss's bulldozers and letting them experience a bit of traffic vibration themselves.

Then, as he always did, Bob thought of Mark and Daryl and calmed down.

He had two young blokes inside and they were both top of their classes and they'd both be top of their universities and professions and they'd both end up living in great big houses in streets so quiet you could hear a hundred dollar note drop.

Bob smiled the smile of a happy man.

Mark chose his moment carefully. He waited till dinner was over and he and Daryl were doing their homework at the kitchen table and Bob was relaxing with the paper and a cup of tea.

Then, heart pounding, he slid the project out from under his folder and across the table towards Bob.

The D was so big and red Mark half expected a siren to go off.

A siren did go off.

Mark jumped, then realized it was an ambulance going past outside.

Probably Rufus, he thought. Must have decided to tell his Mum tonight after all.

Mark held his breath and waited for Bob to look up and see the project.

Bob jumped to his feet.

'Almost forgot,' he said. 'Picked these up for you on the way home.'

Bob rummaged inside his lunch box and pulled out several glossy brochures, which he tossed onto the table on top of the project.

'There you go, champs,' he said.

The red D disappeared under an expensive red car.

'Saab,' said Daryl. 'Beauty.'

Mark watched Daryl grab the top brochure with the carefree enthusiasm of a kid still at primary school who'd never had a D in his life.

At the sink, Joy turned and frowned.

'Bob,' she said, 'they're trying to do their homework.'

'Just giving them a helping hand,' said Bob. 'Reminding them what all the hard slog's for. Even geniuses need to know what they're busting the brainbox for.'

Mark slid the project out from under the brochures and pushed it towards Bob.

'Dad . . .' he said.

But Bob had turned to Joy and was putting his
arms around her.

'Do you want 'em to be doctors and lawyers,' he
said, 'or do you want 'em to end up doing what I do?'

'Farting in the bathroom,' muttered Daryl behind
his brochure.

'Daryl,' said Joy.

Bob bounded over to Daryl, eyes wide with mock
outrage.

'How dare you? I'll have you know, Daryl Top-Of-
The-Class Smalley, that pong was the aftershave
your Mum gave me for Christmas.'

'You liar,' laughed Joy.

Mark slid the project closer to Bob. It was almost
touching his leg.

'Dad . . .'

But Bob was in full flight. He struck his Famous
Lawyer pose and turned to Mark.

'Mark Top-Of-The-Class Smalley, you'll back me
up. Was or was not that duff pong in the bathroom
Santa's aftershave?'

Suddenly Mark didn't have the energy to go
through with it anymore. His last bit of energy was
used up in a flash of anger.

He grabbed the project and stuffed it inside his
folder and slammed the folder shut so hard the
sugar bowl jumped off the table.

The others stared at him.

'Mark,' said Joy, concerned, 'I know you're trying
to work but that's a bit uncalled for. I don't know

where you get that temper from, certainly not your father or me.'

'The milkman,' muttered Daryl.

'Daryl,' yelled Joy.

Bob sat down and ruffled Mark's hair and spoke softly.

'He's okay, just a bit tense. Tough at the top, eh mate? Take it from me, it's going to be worth it. You blokes are going to be somebodies.'

He picked up one of the Saab brochures and put it down in front of Mark.

'Three of these each,' said Bob. Then he grinned. 'Not the brochures, the cars.'

'Yes, Dad,' said Mark sadly.

But he knew it wasn't true.

There'd never be a Saab in his life now.

3

Next morning, walking into school, Mark saw a Saab parked out the front. Climbing out of it was a kid in his class, Annie Upton, a tall, skinny girl with glasses who'd hardly spoken a word to him all year.

Mark watched her untangle her reddy-brown hair from her glasses.

He'd thought all along she was a bit of a snob and now he'd seen her car he was sure of it.

He noticed the woman sitting in the driver's seat. She was wearing a bright yellow sailing jacket and her hair was tied up with a strip of gold cloth and she had dark red nail polish on.

Mark tried to imagine Mum driving a Saab wearing a sailing jacket and nail polish.

He couldn't.

Upton was pleading with the woman.

'Mum,' she said, 'please. I'll just read quietly, I won't be any trouble.'

Mark saw Upton's mum glance at an impressive-looking sailor's watch, one of the ones that was probably also a compass and a sextant and a depth-finder.

'Darling,' she said, 'you know we can't concentrate with you hanging around on the boat. Anyway, you like excursions. Have fun.'

She pulled the door shut, smiled, waved, and drove off.

Upton stood and watched the Saab disappear and looked so unhappy that Mark found himself thinking that perhaps he'd been a bit unfair to her. He'd hardly spoken a word to her all year either.

He went over.

'Parents can be real pains,' he said, 'eh?'

Upton turned and looked at him.

'Yeah,' she said, 'almost as much as boys.'

She walked into school.

An empty flavoured milk carton hit him in the side of the neck and Pino and Rufus came over.

'Don't talk to her,' said Pino, 'she's up herself.'

'Yeah,' said Mark, 'I know.'

Mark struggled to concentrate as Mr Cruickshank wrote the topic for the new project on the board. It wasn't easy because Mr Cruickshank's chalk was squeaking painfully and most of the other kids were mucking up.

Mark almost told them to shut up.

Suddenly, with a theatrical gesture, Mr Cruickshank scrunched up the piece of paper he was copying from.

'Okay,' he shouted, 'if you're not interested . . .'

He pulled out a cigarette lighter and set fire to the scrunched-up piece of paper, holding it above his head like a burning torch.

The class stared at him.

Great, thought Mark, the big project of the year, my last chance to get a good grade, and Cruickshank goes loony and burns the school down.

Mr Cruickshank smiled a weary smile and dropped the burning paper into the waste bin.

'Good,' he said. 'Now I've got your attention, everyone copy this down.' He turned to the board and read out what he'd written. 'You are a famous person in history. Write a letter to a friend or relative telling them about your life.'

As he copied this into his folder, Mark groaned to himself. Another one of Mr Cruickshank's complicated projects. Why couldn't he give them something simple, like Do A Project About Bushrangers?

He glanced over to see what Pino and Rufus thought of the new project. Pino was frowning, tongue sticking out as he wrote. Rufus was shaking his pen and banging it on the desk. Mark could see he hadn't written anything.

When, thought Mark, is Rufus's mum going to stop buying him those crook pens?

Mark took a spare pen from his pencil case. He looked up and saw that Mr Cruickshank was facing the board, tidying up a couple of his f's.

'Today's excursion to the National Treasures Exhibition,' Mr Cruickshank was saying, 'is to help you choose your famous person.'

Mark crouched low and crept over to Rufus's desk. He noticed Upton looking at him as he went, and stuck his tongue out at her.

'This project,' Mr Cruickshank went on, 'carries marks in English and Social Studies as well as

History. It is, as I've said several times, the big one.'

Mark gave Rufus the pen and didn't wait for Rufus's relieved grin of thanks. He was halfway back to his desk when he realized Mr Cruickshank was staring at him.

'I hope,' said Mr Cruickshank grimly, 'that little conversation was about history, Smalley.'

'Um . . .'

Mark was about to explain about Rufus's pen when he remembered that Mr Cruickshank had warned Rufus several times about bringing sub-standard pens to school.

'Smalley,' said Mr Cruickshank, raising his voice, 'was that conversation about history?'

'Yes sir,' said Mark.

'Good,' said Mr Cruickshank, 'then you can share it with the rest of us.'

Mark's brain went like the telly when a big truck was going past. He tried to remember something they'd done in history, anything, but all he could think of was pens and bushrangers, and bush-rangers was primary.

He looked desperately around the room.

On the wall next to his desk was the poster Mr Cruickshank had put up earlier. 'See Phar Lap,' it said, 'At The National Treasures Exhibition, Limited Season Only, State Museum.' There was a picture of the famous racehorse and a newspaper headline saying '1929 Melbourne Cup'.

Mark heard himself speaking.

'I was telling Wainwright who won the 1929 Melbourne Cup, sir.'

He glanced round and saw that Rufus was looking puzzled.

Mr Cruickshank looked at Mark. 'I hope you told him correctly,' he said, 'because if you didn't you can spend today picking up litter on the oval. Both of you.'

Mark's heart was pounding.

'Phar Lap, sir,' he said.

Mr Cruickshank gave a weary sigh. 'Off you go, Smalley. And you, Wainwright. Take this to Mr Savage.' He sat at his desk and started scribbling a note.

Mark felt hot and angry. His last chance for a decent grade down the dunny because the stupid poster was wrong.

Then he felt someone poking him in the back.

He spun round.

Upton was holding something out to him. A piece of paper.

He took it and looked at it. '1929 Nightmarch,' it said, '1930 Phar Lap.'

He stared at her. She nodded.

'Sorry, sir,' said Mark, turning to Mr Cruickshank who was still scribbling, 'I'm thinking of 1930. The winner of the 1929 Melbourne Cup was Nightmarch.'

Mr Cruickshank stopped and looked hard at Mark.

Then, with another weary sigh, he screwed up what he'd been writing and dropped it into the bin.

As the class filed across the playground towards the bus, Mark realized Annie Upton wasn't with them. He went to find her.

She was still at her locker. Mark came up behind her and cleared his throat.

'Thanks,' he said. 'How do you know all that stuff?'

She spun round, startled, and slammed her locker door. As she did, Mark saw the inside was plastered with pictures of horses.

She looked at him steadily.

'I read a lot,' she said.

Mr Cruickshank's voice floated in from outside. 'Straight to the bus, everyone. Wainwright, put that boy down.'

'You'll miss the excursion,' said Annie.

'What about you?' said Mark. 'Aren't you going?'

Annie shook her head and turned away.

'Do you chuck on buses?' asked Mark. Daryl chucked on buses sometimes.

Annie looked at him.

'There's something at the museum I don't want to see,' she said quietly.

Mark nodded. He knew how she felt. 'Yeah,' he said, 'I don't much like the guts in bottles either.'

Annie gave a small smile but Mark could tell there was something more than guts in bottles bothering her.

The door to the playground flew open and Mr Cruickshank burst in, hot and breathless. He glared at them.

'Smalley. Upton. On the bus.'

Annie's shoulders sagged as she walked past Mark towards the bus.

■ 18 ■

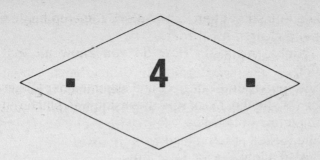

4

'What about Batman?' said Rufus as they straggled into the museum. 'He's a famous figure from history.'

'He's not real, dummy,' said Pino. 'He's just Bruce Wayne dressed up.'

'He's not dead,' said Mark. 'Shanksie wants us to choose someone who's dead.'

Mr Cruickshank, who was in the middle of explaining to the class that he wanted each of them to choose someone who was dead, stopped and glared at Mark

'Smalley,' he said, 'I would have thought you of all people would have been paying attention seeing as this project is your last chance for a decent grade this year. Or would you rather gossip with Wainwright and Abrozetti and end up a nobody?'

'No sir,' said Mark.

'It's a jungle out there, Smalley,' said Mr Cruickshank, 'and nobodies get gobbled up.'

'Yes sir,' said Mark.

Behind Mr Cruickshank was a glass case full of

large stuffed animals with small stuffed animals in their mouths.

'Yuk,' said Rufus.

'Okay, this way,' said Mr Cruickshank, leading them past a big sign saying 'National Treasures Exhibition'. 'Stay together and I'll point out famous people from history. Abrozetti, you won't get inspired with your finger up your nose.'

Mark didn't get inspired either.

As he wandered around the exhibition he realized that most of the national treasures on display were bits of old-fashioned farm machinery.

With a sinking feeling Mark stared up at a portrait of the grim, black-bearded inventor of a plough that could jump over tree stumps. How could he do a project on someone that grumpy?

He was going to fail this one too.

Pino and Rufus came over and from their faces Mark could tell they were feeling the same.

'What about Dracula?' said Rufus.

'He's not dead, he's just sleeping,' said Pino.

'I reckon it's sick,' said Mark, 'making us write letters from dead people. It could warp our minds. We could end up working in a cemetery.'

Pino and Rufus nodded glumly. Then jumped as Mr Cruickshank's face appeared next to Mark's.

'I take it from all this talk you've chosen your famous person from history?'

'No sir,' said Mark.

'Well, Smalley, I can't make you do well on this project but I can ask you to stop distracting members of the class who do want to use their imagination.'

Mr Cruickshank turned back to the rest of the class and pointed to a painting of some eighteenth-century sailors landing on a beach.

'Now,' he said, 'who's decided to be Captain Cook? Anyone?'

Half the class put their hands up. Pino and Rufus looked at each other and raised their hands as well.

Mr Cruickshank sighed wearily and, for the ninth time that week, wished he'd become a dentist like his grandfather.

Mark walked slowly away from the others. This is hopeless, he thought. How can I be expected to get back the top of the class and be a somebody with dumb projects like this?

He started thinking about running away from home and getting a job in television and becoming a somebody that way.

Then he stopped.

Annie Upton was standing in the next room, frozen, staring at something Mark couldn't see because there was a pillar in the way. Her face was pale and expressionless.

As Mark moved closer he saw something glistening on her cheeks. Tears.

Concerned, he moved closer still, past the pillar, until he could see what she was looking at.

The body of a horse. A huge reddy-brown horse, perfectly preserved, standing on a raised platform. With a sign saying 'Phar Lap. On Loan From The Victorian Museum'.

That's a bit crook, thought Mark, having a dead horse where kids who like horses can see it and get upset.

He stood next to Annie.

'Are you okay?' he asked softly.

Annie didn't answer, didn't take her eyes off Phar Lap.

Gawking tourists were leaning over the security rope, peering at the horse's massive body.

A woman pointed to the veins bulging on Phar Lap's legs.

'Bit like me before I had mine done,' she said to her friend.

A little boy pointed to Phar Lap's groin.

'Look, Mummy,' he said loudly, 'big willy.'

Mark looked at Annie again. She was still expressionless, but another tear was running down her cheek.

Mark was just wondering what he should do when Pino and Rufus emerged from behind a bale of wool and stared at Annie.

'Hey, Upton,' said Pino, 'it's okay, it won't bite you.'

'It's only a horse,' said Rufus.

Annie turned to them, her bottom lip quivering.

'It's not just a horse,' she said. 'It's the best racehorse in the history of Australia. The whole of Australia loved this horse. The whole world did.'

She was yelling now, and Pino and Rufus were staring at her. So were the tourists.

Fifty-one races, thirty-seven wins,' shouted Annie. 'Fourteen wins in a row from September the thirteenth, 1930, to March the fourth, 1931.'

Mr Cruickshank strode over.

'Upton, what's the matter? Are you sick?'

'Reckon,' said Pino.

Panting and tearful, Annie glared at Pino and Mr Cruickshank, then ran towards the door.

Mr Cruickshank started to go after her.

Mark grabbed his arm.

'Sir ... sir ... it's okay,' he said, thinking frantically. 'Her ... um ... grandmother was bitten by a horse. And she died. At the races.' He looked up anxiously to see if Mr Cruickshank was buying it. He seemed to be.

'I'll go outside with her,' said Mark.

Mr Cruickshank looked at him darkly.

'I think you'd better,' he said.

Mark ran out of the museum and saw Annie standing near the bus. He went over.

'He was dead when they stuffed him,' said Mark gently. 'Phar Lap can't feel a thing.'

Annie stared at the ground.

'Yes, I can,' she said, so softly Mark wasn't even sure he'd heard right.

'What do you mean?' he asked.

Annie still didn't look up.

'Forget it,' she muttered. 'You and your numbskull mates'd just think it's a big joke.'

Mark wondered what she was on about.

'No, we wouldn't,' he said. 'Not if you tell us what's going on.'

Annie breathed in and breathed out and looked up at the sky.

Mark had an eerie thought.

'Listen,' he said, 'you're not, you know, mental and stuff? It's okay, I won't tell anyone.'

Annie spun round to face him, suddenly angry and tearful again.

'I'm Phar Lap,' she yelled. 'It's my body.'

Mark stared at her.

He couldn't have heard that right.

Annie took a deep breath.

'I'm the reincarnation of Phar Lap,' she said quietly.

There was a silence while Mark tried to work out exactly what she meant.

'Reincarnation means when you die you come back as someone else,' said Annie.

Mark looked at her, wondering if she was joking.

He could see she wasn't.

He remembered the video he'd seen at Pino's where some radioactive chemicals were spilled in a graveyard and all the dead bodies came to life and went to McDonalds.

'Is that why some people have really bad skin?' he said.

Annie sighed.

'You leave your old body behind,' she said. 'You're born with a new body and your old spirit.'

Mark wondered how he could get back into the museum without looking rude.

'Everyone's a reincarnation,' said Annie. She pointed to the people walking past on the street. 'All these people have been something else in a past life. Kings. Explorers . . .'

'Hey, Smalley,' called a voice. It was a couple of the kids from class peeking out of the museum door. 'You going to be a male nurse?'

'. . . Burrowing reptiles,' continued Annie, glaring at them. 'Everyone's been someone else before. Including you.'

Mark was still admiring the burrowing reptiles' reply, so it took him a moment to realize what she'd said after that.

'Me?' said Mark.

This was getting crazier by the minute.

'Perhaps that's why I like carrots so much,' he heard himself saying. "Cause I was a rabbit.'

Annie glared at him.

'Yeah, yeah,' she said, 'big joke, ha ha.'

She walked away angrily.

Mark decided not to go after her.

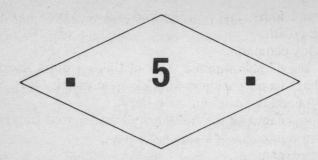

5

That night Mark sat at the kitchen table trying to get started on the new project.

He read the topic for the forty-eighth time: 'You Are A Famous Person In History. Write A Letter To A Friend Or Relative Telling Them About Your Life'.

For the nineteenth time he flipped through the encyclopaedia.

It was hopeless.

How could he be a famous person in history when he couldn't even be a famous person in school any more?

Mark closed the encyclopaedia and sighed.

Daryl looked over from the open door of the freezer, where he was standing eating ice cream straight out of the container.

'You could tell Dad you banged your head on the wardrobe door and got brain damage,' he said.

Mark looked at Daryl wearily, making a mental note that it was a mistake to tell younger brothers when you got a D.

Daryl shrugged. 'That's what I told Dad when

I came fourth last year,' he said and went back to the ice cream.

Joy came in.

'Daryl!' she shouted. 'Out of there. I don't know what this obsession is with ice cream lately.'

'I need the calcium,' said Daryl.

Joy slammed the freezer door and tossed Daryl's spoon into the sink with a clatter.

Bob came in.

'Hey, keep it down,' he said. 'There's a bloke in here knocking together a prize-winning project.'

Joy resisted the temptation to yell at Bob. He was right, Mark was trying to work. She let Bob steer her and Daryl out of the kitchen.

Bob ruffled Mark's hair.

'Show 'em what you're made of, champ,' he said.

As Bob went back into the lounge room he thought of Mark onstage at the high school prize-giving in a couple of months and suddenly the mortgage interest rate increase that Joy was in the middle of telling him about didn't seem so bad after all.

Mark looked at the encyclopaedia on the table in front of him. Then he opened it. He didn't flick through it this time, he turned the pages purpose-fully until he came to the word he was looking for.

Reincarnation.

When Mark saw Annie's house, he almost turned round and went home again.

It was two storeys, white, with a white wrought-iron balcony. The front garden was full of giant ferns. An old-fashioned brass lamp over the gate gleamed in the morning sun. The street number was brass too. Or gold.

Mark took a deep breath, pushed the gate open, went up to the front door and knocked loudly with the brass or gold knocker.

He waited, wondering what he'd say if Mrs Upton opened the door. Small talk about sailing would be best. He'd tell her about the time Daryl fell out of the pedal-o boat and ripped his —

The door opened. It was Annie. She looked surprised, then suspicious.

'What are you doing here?' she said.

'I want to talk to you,' said Mark. 'About reincarnation.

Annie scowled. She stepped past him, turned on a hose and sprayed it into the ferns.

'Okay Wainwright, okay Abrozetti,' she shouted, 'come out and have your laugh and then rack off.'

'It's just me,' said Mark. 'I just want to ask you a couple of things.'

Annie looked at him for a long time, still spraying the ferns. Then she turned the hose off.

Mark couldn't take his eyes off Annie's walls.

They were covered with Phar Lap stuff. Posters, old photos, drawings, articles cut out of magazines, photocopies of newspaper stories.

Would anyone else except Phar Lap, he thought, go to this much trouble?

He realized she'd finished telling him how reincarnation was a big part of several major and important religions in the world. It was time for the biggie.

'If I was someone else before I was born,' he said, 'how come I can't remember anything about it?'

'Can you remember being born?' she asked.

Mark tried. He couldn't.

'So it stands to reason,' she said, 'you can't remember stuff that happened before that.'

Mark felt a shiver run down his back.

Time for the other biggie.

'How did you find out who you were?' he asked.

'It just sort of came to me. Phar Lap was incredibly popular, right, the whole country loved him, so it stands to reason.'

'What does?' said Mark.

Mrs Upton's voice floated up from downstairs.

'Annie, Dad and I are going sailing. Your pasta's in the microwave.'

Mark heard the front door slam.

Annie fiddled with the carpet for a bit.

'I'm having this life to stop me getting big-headed,' she said quietly. 'That's why my olds don't give a stuff about me.'

Mark waited to see if she wanted to say any more about that.

She didn't seem to.

'How did it just sort of come to you?' he asked.

Annie grinned at him. 'You want to find out who you are, don't you?'

Mark felt his face getting hot. 'No ... I'm just sort of ... you know ... interested.'

He could see she didn't believe him.

'You've really got to want to know,' said Annie. 'I really wanted to know. Then it just sort of came to me.'

'How?'

Annie took something from her bookshelf and held it out. It was a video movie. *Phar Lap*.

'While I was watching this.'

6

The video shop manager stared as the pile of videos on legs tottered towards him down the aisle.

He'd seen kids stock up for the weekend plenty of times before, but never with this many.

Interesting selection of titles too.

Gandhi, *Amadeus*, *Burke and Wills*, *Greystoke The Legend of Tarzan*, *Lawrence of Arabia*, *Frankenstein*, *Patton*, *Jimi Hendrix*, *Lenny*, *Ned Kelly*, *Golda*, *Isadora*, *W.C. Fields and Me*, *Lassie*.

Mark's face peered over the top of the pile.

'I'll take these, thanks,' he said.

'I'll need some proof of who you are,' said the manager.

'I'll let you know when I've watched them,' said Mark.

Thirty-six hours later Mark had watched them.

He rolled away from the television, looked at the video boxes and cassettes scattered around him on the floor, and groaned.

Fourteen movies and the only thing that had come to him was a headache.

During *Tarzan* he'd felt the back of his neck prickling and for a moment he'd thought it was a sign until he realized he was lying on an old biscuit.

Mark groaned again.

He saw Daryl standing in the doorway staring at him.

'Nothing?' said Daryl, eyes wide with disbelief. 'Fourteen movies and not a single tit?'

Mark sighed.

Bob appeared in the doorway behind Daryl. He looked at all the video boxes and frowned.

'You're sure all this is for the project?' he said.

'Yes, Dad,' said Mark wearily.

He sighed again.

Now Daryl was winking at him.

Later that evening Mark had an idea.

He rummaged around until he found the old photo album, then studied his baby photos closely.

No good.

The only person he looked a tiny bit like was Elton John, and Elton John wasn't even dead yet.

Mark went into the kitchen.

'Mum,' he said, 'when I was a baby, did I remind you of anyone?'

Joy thought for a bit, then smiled fondly at Mark.

'Porky Pig.'

The playground was full of kids tearing about and shouting and pushing and not behaving one bit like recycled adults.

Must be all the sugar we eat, thought Mark.

Then he saw Annie walking towards the main building. He ran over to her.

'It didn't work,' he said breathlessly. 'I watched heaps of movies and nothing happened.'

She didn't even stop walking, just glared at him.

'You and your mates can drop dead,' she said, and walked twice as fast.

Mark walked with her, not knowing what to say.

Hope I don't turn out to be a horse, he thought, I'd hate to be that temperamental.

Then he heard Pino and Rufus behind them, giggling.

'Seriously but,' Pino called out to Annie, 'do you sleep standing up?'

Annie turned, glared at them, then at Mark again.

Mark decided it was time he had a talk with Pino about reincarnation and manners. He sprinted over, jumped on Pino's back and they both crashed to the ground.

The school library was full of kids pretending to be Famous People In History. Some with more success than others.

As Mr Cruickshank strolled among the bowed heads and moving pens, he was pleased to see that most folders had at least half a page of project in them already.

Most, but not all.

Mr Cruickshank frowned as he stood over Rufus Wainwright, who was sucking his pen, deep in thought.

'Dear Mum,' Rufus had written, 'Guess what? I'm Batman.' Batman was crossed out. So were the other names that followed it. Allan Border. Indiana Jones. God.

Mr Cruickshank moved along to Pino Abrozetti, who had written even less. 'To Whom It May Concern' was the sum total of his efforts so far, if you didn't count the intergalactic motorbike he'd drawn on his pencil case.

And here was Mark Smalley, who hadn't written a thing, staring into space.

Mr Cruickshank thought about having words with Smalley. Then he remembered the article he'd read in the holidays about how some kids were hopeless students because of their genes. He moved on to the next table.

'Thought he'd never go,' Mark whispered to the others, sliding the book out from under his folder.

'What's that?' asked Rufus, looking at the book.

Mark showed him the cover: *Reincarnation Revealed – Discover Your Past Lives*.

Mark had already decided it was the best book he'd ever read, worth every cent of the $1.95 he'd paid in the second-hand bookshop. It also had the information he needed now that Upton wasn't talking to him.

'Reincarnation's a con,' whispered Rufus. 'I saw it on telly. You and Upton have been conned.'

'Do you believe everything you see on telly?' whispered Mark.

'Yeah,' said Rufus. 'Except the news.'

Pino leant over and looked at the page Mark was reading. He saw the word Mark had underlined.

'What's a seance?' he whispered.

'It's getting in touch with dead people,' whispered Mark, 'to find out who you were before.'

'Yuk,' said Pino.

He said it quite loudly, so they all pretended to write for a while in case Mr Cruickshank had heard.

'If you've lived before,' whispered Pino after a bit, 'how come you're not all green and mouldy?'

''Cause you get a new body each life, dummo,' whispered Mark.

'Gee,' muttered Pino, 'I wonder if I could come back as Deidre Armitage in 5B?'

Mark saw Mr Cruickshank looking at them and they all scribbled stuff on their pencil cases for a couple of minutes.

Then Rufus whispered to Mark. 'Why are you doing this?'

'I want to find out if I'm a somebody,' said Mark quietly.

Rufus and Pino thought about this for a moment.

'Course you're not a somebody,' whispered Rufus. 'You're a kid.'

'But what if we've all been somebodies in a past life,' said Mark. 'Don't you want to find out if you've done great deeds? Won great victories? Travelled great journeys?'

Rufus and Pino shook their heads.

'I might have caught something,' said Pino.

'Don't you want to get top marks in the project?' asked Mark.

Rufus and Pino thought about this.

'What's reincarnation got to do with the project?' asked Rufus.

'Look how much Upton's written,' said Mark.

They all leaned back to the table behind them and had a peek at Annie's folder.

'Dear Mum and Dad,' her first page began, 'you know me as Annie, but I am actually Phar Lap . . .'

She was already halfway through her second page.

Rufus and Pino's eyes widened.

'Smalley, Wainwright, Abrozetti,' hissed Mr Cruickshank across the library, 'do your own work.'

They hunched over their pencil cases and scribbled frantically for five minutes.

Then Rufus leaned over to Mark.

'This seance,' he whispered, 'when are you doing it?'

'Tonight,' said Mark.

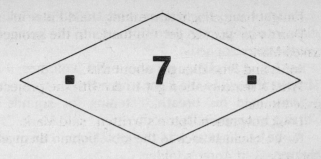

7

Mark finished the reincarnation book under the bed covers by torchlight. Then he read the seance chapter again, just to make sure he'd got all the details right.

When he'd done that he looked at his watch.

Seven past midnight.

Time to go.

He got dressed as quietly as he could. The batteries were going in the torch and in the dull light the footballers on his wall seemed to be watching him with strange expressions on their faces.

They probably know, thought Mark, that after tonight I'll be swapping them for someone else.

Mark decided to do the difficult bit first.

He crept into Daryl's room. Daryl was asleep with his feet hanging off the side of the bed and his head on a Lego spaceship.

Fortunately it wasn't Daryl's Lego that Mark had come for, it was his Scrabble.

Mark found it on the floor in the corner, picked the box up carefully so it wouldn't rattle, and crept out of the room.

He went into the kitchen and stuffed a drinking glass into his pocket, then tiptoed into the lounge to get the encyclopaedia.

As he was piling up the eight volumes, one slipped and fell to the floor with a thud.

Mark held his breath, listening for sounds of stirring in his parents' room.

All he could hear was the occasional car on the flyover.

It was only after he'd piled up the encyclopaedia, put the Scrabble box on top, picked them all up and turned to leave that he saw Daryl standing in the doorway watching him.

The street next to the cemetery was empty except for Mark, Pino, several parked cars and Daryl.

'I reckon the whole idea's childish,' said Daryl, clutching the Scrabble box to his chest and nervously eyeing the dark bits of street between the street lights.

Pino shifted his four volumes of encyclopaedia to his other arm and gave Mark a look.

Mark wasn't sure if the look meant 'why did you bring him?' 'why did you bring such a heavy encyclopaedia?' or 'when's Rufus getting here?'

'Why did you bring him?' hissed Pino.

'I had to,' whispered Mark, 'it's his Scrabble.'

'Stupid and childish,' said Daryl. 'Reincarnation's what they have in those dumb horror movies.'

A dark shape loomed out of the shadows next to him.

'Arghhhh!' said Daryl.

'Sorry I'm late,' said Rufus, 'Mum's new boyfriend went for a swim at the beach today and he kept getting up with gastric.'

'What's the plan?' asked Pino.

'Simple,' said Mark, 'we just go into the cemetery and have a seance.'

'Does the book say it's got to be in a cemetery?' asked Rufus. He was looking nervously at the shadows now.

'Not exactly,' said Mark, 'I just thought it'd be a good place to make contact with the departed.'

'What about a phone box?' said Daryl.

Mark ignored him.

As they went down the street towards the cemetery gates, Mark found himself glancing into the shadows and wondering if the cemetery was such a good idea after all.

And when they got to the gates and found they were padlocked, nobody suggested climbing over.

Which was just as well because half a minute later headlights beamed through the dark onto the gates.

They all ducked down behind the bushes just in time, and watched a security car cruise slowly past.

'We'll have to find somewhere else,' said Mark.

'Don't be dumb,' said Pino, 'where else can you have a seance at this time of night?'

'It's very bright in here,' said Rufus.

'Of course it's bright,' said Mark. 'It's a laundromat. Laundromats are always bright. It's so you can see if your washing's clean.'

Mark found a bit of cardboard from a washing

powder box and tore it in half. He wrote 'yes' on one bit and 'no' on the other and put them down on the lid of a washing machine. He placed the drinking glass between them, upside down.

'Great place for making contact with the departed,' said Daryl sarcastically.

Mark found himself wondering how much younger brothers shrank if you washed them on the hot cycle.

'As a matter of fact it's an excellent place for making contact with the departed,' said Mark. 'When a person dies they usually leave a bit of dirty washing behind. Stands to reason their spirits'll be down here making sure the relatives don't forget to put the fabric softener in.'

Mark put one fingertip onto the upturned glass.

'Okay,' he said, 'let's start.'

The others all gathered round and put one finger each onto the glass.

'This is crazy,' said Pino.

'Concentrate,' said Mark, 'and no pushing.'

He decided to do Pino first in the hope of cutting down on the whinging. Mark raised his voice, taking on a tone he hoped was right for talking to fussy spirits.

'Has Pino Abrozetti lived before?'

'Can't we do me first?' asked Rufus. 'Mum always gets up for a pee at two o'clock.'

'Shhhh,' said Pino.

'Has Pino Abrozetti had a past life?' intoned Mark.

Suddenly the washing machine burst into life and started to vibrate.

Slowly the glass slid over to 'yes'.

'It's working,' shouted Pino.

Incredible, thought Mark. None of us started that machine, and there's nobody else here.

He grabbed the Scrabble box, pulled open the door of a spin dryer and tipped the plastic letters in. Then he closed the door, put twenty cents in the slot and watched the letters clatter about inside.

'Oh great,' said Daryl. 'That's very good for them.'

Mark pulled open the door and all the letters fell to the bottom of the dryer.

'Choose your letters,' said Mark.

Pino closed his eyes and grabbed a handful of letters. He put them on a washing machine lid and they all excitedly turned them over.

'Now,' said Mark. 'A name.'

They all slid the letters around, searching for a name.

'Zirp,' said Pino.

'Trud,' said Rufus.

'Silt,' said Daryl.

There was a long pause while they all studied the letters again.

'Wait,' said Mark, 'I've got it.'

Excitedly he rearranged the letters.

'Aurelitus!' cried Mark. 'He was an emperor of Rome, I'm sure of it!'

He grabbed the A-to-D volume of the encyclopaedia.

'An emperor,' said Pino, gazing majestically at the distant washing-powder dispenser.

'Cruickshank'll have to call you Your Serene Highness,' said Rufus.

Mark found the page and ran his finger down the

column. 'Aurelitus . . . Aurelitus.'

There it was!

'Aurelitus,' read Mark out loud, 'a toxic fungus mainly found on the droppings of ruminants.'

They looked at each other, then at the encyclopaedia, then at each other again.

'Can't wait to read the project,' said Daryl.

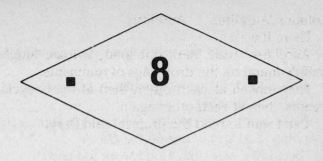

8

'Shake a leg,' said Bob, 'It's seven-thirty.'
Mark forced his eyes open.

He felt crook, as if he'd only had about five hours sleep. Then he remembered he had only had about five hours sleep.

'It's a brand new day,' Bob was saying, 'and it's a beauty. Think of all the things you can do in a brand new day.'

Mark knew the thing he was going to do. Take that dumb book back and get a refund.

He stumbled past Bob and into the bathroom.

Bob watched him, worried by how tired he looked. Daryl looked the same.

Must be tough on the poor little blokes, thought Bob. All that effort they put into coming top. Still, school year's nearly over and then they'll have the holidays.

He decided to make himself a bit late and give them both a lift to school. They deserved it and he could give them a bit of a pep talk on the way.

Mark hurried out of the house, still chewing his toast.

Bob and Daryl were already in the car and the engine was running.

Mark went over to Joy, who was watering her saplings, and kissed her on the cheek.

'Bye, love,' said Joy. 'Don't work too hard.'

Mark got into the car.

'Okay, champs,' said Bob, 'let's go out there and knock their socks off.'

There was a loud thump and suddenly the outside of the windscreen was covered in brown liquid and what looked like bits of chicken skin.

They got out.

A soggy Kentucky Fried Chicken box was slowly sliding off the bonnet. A dented Coke can lay on the roof, dribbling. Chicken scraps were splattered all over the front of the car.

They looked up at the flyover.

'Some mongrel chucked it over,' said Bob angrily.

'Scumbags,' yelled Daryl.

Over by the saplings Joy was standing with the hose, staring up at the flyover.

'Pigs,' she said. 'Sooner these trees grow and give us some privacy the better.'

She came over and started hosing the car down.

'Mark, Daryl, listen to me,' said Bob. 'You can be one of two things in this life.' He pointed up at the flyover. 'You can be the bloke who builds that . . . or,' he pointed to the mess on the car, 'you can be the bloke who cops this.'

Oh well, thought Mark miserably, s'pose I'd better get myself a garbage-proof umbrella.

Bulldozers roared. Walls toppled. Dust swirled. Men shouted.

The noise was deafening.

They stood at the edge of the demolition site, watching bits of the old building come crashing down.

Bob squinted, grim-faced.

Daryl stared, fascinated.

Mark frowned, puzzled.

Dad had brought them to sites before, but never on the way to school.

Perhaps he knows, thought Mark. Perhaps he knows reincarnation's a con and I'm going to fail the big assignment. Perhaps he's getting me used to demolition sites 'cause he knows I'll end up working on them like him.

Mark realized Bob was saying something.

'Every day of my life,' yelled Bob, 'I wish my Mum and Dad had made me get a decent education. Do you know what makes it okay, working in a crook place like this? Knowing you blokes are going to be like him.'

Mark saw that Bob was pointing to a gleaming dark blue Mercedes that was pulling up nearby.

'A somebody,' said Bob.

A man in a suit got out of the back of the Mercedes and Mark could tell from the way he stood and pointed at things while other men scurried around him that he was pretty important.

The man glanced at his watch.

Probably owns a few other sites as well, thought Mark, and wants to go and boss people around on all of them before lunch.

Then Mark saw how Bob was looking at the man, and suddenly he felt a lump in his chest.

He wanted Dad to look at him that way.

'Somebodies do it,' said Bob, 'ordinary folk get it done to them.' He put his arms round Mark and Daryl and squeezed them. 'Mates, I would have been so disappointed if you two had turned out ordinary.'

Mark decided to give reincarnation one more try.

The woman had such a nice smile that Mark knew it was going to work out this time.

The room was nice too. It had brightly coloured pieces of cloth on the walls and posters of rainforests.

Mark wondered if a person could be a rainforest in a past life.

'What can I do for you?' asked the woman.

Mark noticed the tiny plaits in her hair had coloured feathers in them.

She must have budgies.

'Your ad in the health food shop said you do past lives hypnosis,' he said.

'That's right.'

She gave him another nice smile.

Mark reached into his pocket and pulled out his money and put it on the table between them.

'I'm afraid past lives hypnosis is $80 a session,' she said, still smiling.

'This is all I've got,' said Mark.

Eighty dollars. He'd be dead and onto his next life before he could save up that much.

'I'm sorry,' she said, still smiling.

In the next room a wind-chime tinkled softly.

'Would you show me how to do it myself for $7.40?' said Mark.

Mark yawned and propped himself up higher in bed and read the same bit for the third time.

This book was nowhere near as easy to read as the reincarnation one. That woman should have warned him before she sold it to him.

'Self-hypnosis,' he read, 'is a way into the subconscious, the part of us that knows who we really are.'

Mark yawned again. If only he wasn't so tired after last night.

He read on. 'But the subconscious doesn't speak to us directly. We have to look for clues, particularly when we wake from a deep sleep.'

Deep sleep, he understood that bit.

He closed the book.

Okay, he thought, let's give it a go.

He picked up a small box covered in velvet and opened it. Inside, lying on more velvet, was a small spoon.

Mark took it out.

On the end of the handle was a metal badge with the name of his primary school on it. Underneath the badge, on the handle, were carved his name and the words Dux Of The School.

Mark took a deep breath and held the spoon out at arms length and looked at the other end, the curved bit.

He could see his face, reflected, tiny.

It looked like the face of someone who'd never tried to hypnotize himself and was about to now.

Slowly he moved the spoon towards his staring eyes, swinging it from side to side.

As the spoon came closer his reflection began to change.

By the time the spoon was halfway to his face he couldn't recognize himself any more.

9

'**C**ome on, Mark!' called Joy. 'It's seven-thirty!'
Mark groaned and started to open his eyes.
Then he stopped.

He could feel his Dux spoon between his cheek and the pillow, and the self-hypnosis book under his tummy.

Self-hypnosis.

Had it worked?

He couldn't remember.

All he could remember was a bit from the book: 'We have to look for clues, particularly when we wake from a deep sleep.'

Okay, thought Mark, here goes.

One, two, three.

He opened his eyes.

All he could see was Daryl, standing in the wardrobe eating ice cream out of the plastic tub with his fingers.

'Daryl,' he croaked, 'do that in your own room.'

'Remember the deal,' said Daryl, coming over to the bed. 'You don't say anything about ice cream,

I don't say anything about laundromats.'

Daryl was standing right next to Mark now, with the ice cream tub close to Mark's face.

A clue, thought Mark, I'm looking for a clue.

He wondered if a person could be ice cream in a past life.

Then he saw the label on the ice cream tub.

A picture of snow-covered mountains and blue water. And one word.

Fjord.

'Fjord,' said Mark.

'What?' said Daryl.

'Fjord,' said Mark.

From outside came the sound of the old Falcon revving and spluttering as Bob set off for work.

'What,' said Daryl, grinning, 'you mean Dad in the Fjord Falcon?'

Mark sat upright, suddenly wide awake.

'That's it!' he cried. 'Ford! That must be it! Ford!'

He leapt out of bed and rushed out to the lounge.

'Great,' said Daryl, staring after him, 'my brother's the reincarnation of a village idiot.'

Henry Ford.

Mark sat under the high vaulted ceiling of the State Library and the silence of the huge room roared in his ears like applause.

When he'd looked in the encyclopaedia at home and seen who Henry Ford was he'd hardly been able to believe it, so he'd come into the State Library where he knew they'd have the most reliable books to double check.

Mark stared at the pile of books on the leather-topped desk in front of him.

All of them about Henry Ford.

On the front of one was an old black-and-white photo of a man in a funny-looking suit standing outside a funny-looking factory next to a long line of funny-looking old-fashioned cars.

The man didn't look funny, though. The way he stood was the way the man with the Mercedes had stood.

Mark took a deep breath, opened the book, and read the bit inside the front cover.

'Henry Ford,' it said, 'legend ... genius ... one of the wealthiest men of his age ... a hero of the twentieth century ... the man who put the world on wheels.'

It was true.

'Yes!' shouted Mark.

His voice echoed round the huge library.

Elderly readers looked up, startled.

Librarians spun round, annoyed.

Attendants jolted awake, outraged.

Mark didn't notice any of them. He'd turned to chapter one and was reading about what he'd been like as a child.

The bell to end morning break was clanging and the corridor was full of kids hurrying in all directions.

Mark saw Pino and Rufus heading into class. He ran over to them, panting under the weight of his Henry Ford books.

'Pino! Rufus!' he yelled. 'It worked! I know who I am!'

Rufus looked at him warily.

Pino looked at him sourly.

Fair enough, thought Mark, they're a bit suspicious after the seance. Fair enough.

'You can find out who you are,' said Mark. 'You use self-hypnosis. It's easy.'

He thrust the self-hypnosis book at them.

Pino and Rufus didn't look convinced.

'What are you,' said Pino, 'a toadstool or a mushroom?'

They both smirked and walked off.

'I'm Henry Ford,' yelled Mark. 'I invented car factories. I put the world on wheels.'

'That's great,' shouted back Pino. 'My brother-in-law wants a word with you about his exhaust.'

Mark watched, deflated, as Pino and Rufus ran giggling into the classroom.

He'd thought they'd be pleased.

Oh well, give them time to get used to it.

'Now you know what it's like,' said a voice behind him.

Mark turned. Annie was standing looking at him steadily. It was the first time she'd come near him for days.

Mark wondered if Pino and Rufus had been giving her a hard time again and if she was going to blame him again.

Then she grinned.

'G'day, Henry.'

Mark grinned back, relieved.

He was about to start telling her the whole story when another voice rang out.

'Smalley!'

Mr Cruickshank was bearing down on them, face like thunder.

'Smalley, I hope you of all people have got a good reason for missing class this morning.'

'Research, sir,' said Mark.

Mr Cruickshank stopped and stared at the pile of books in Mark's arms. He pulled Mark's folder out of the pile and opened it.

Mark was glad he'd made a start on the project at the library. Now he knew who he was it had been easy. He'd done nearly a page in half an hour.

Mr Cruickshank closed the folder and thought about writing an article next holidays about how good teaching could make any kid into a good student regardless of their genes.

'Well, Smalley,' he said, 'you're a dark horse.'

'No sir,' said Mark, 'that's Upton, sir.'

Mr Cruickshank thought about this. He saw Upton and Smalley grinning at each other.

Eight years I've been a teacher, thought Mr Cruickshank, and I still don't understand kids' jokes.

Mark ran from the bus stop to home, heart pounding with excitement.

Usually the traffic roaring along this stretch gave him a headache, but today all he could hear were two words.

Henry Ford.

He wasn't even seeing the traffic.

What he was seeing was him telling Mum and Dad who he was and Mum and Dad hugging each other with excitement.

And him.

And then Dad looking at him the way he'd looked at the man with the Mercedes.

And then the Ford Motor Company flying them all to America and giving them a guided tour round their car factory in Detroit because, after all, he'd invented it.

Mark burst in through the front gate and saw Joy.

'Mum!' he yelled, 'Guess what . . .'

He stopped.

Joy was kneeling next to the four little trees crunching something in her fingers.

Leaves.

Dead leaves.

She was crying.

Mark stared at the saplings. He'd noticed a couple of days ago they weren't looking too healthy, but they hadn't looked anything like this.

Dead.

He went over and put his arm round Joy. When she saw him she started blinking and frowning and pretending she hadn't been crying.

Mark had never seen her so upset, not even when Daryl had fallen down a drain in Mildura and been stuck there for two hours.

'What happened?' he yelled softly.

She pointed to the traffic roaring past.

'Car fumes got 'em. I must have been kidding myself, thinking anything'd grow here.'

Mark put his books down and hugged her.

She looked up at the flyover howling over their heads.

'Whoever invented cars,' she shouted angrily, 'should be strung up.'

Mark stared at the shrivelled brown saplings, which vibrated slightly each time a car hurtled past.

He looked at the Henry Ford books at his feet.

'What about ... what about the person who invented car factories?' he said softly.

Joy didn't hear him.

He didn't repeat the question.

10

Mark sat on the metal crash barrier up on the flyover and watched the afternoon rush-hour traffic crawl past.

Lines of hot and fuming cars driven by hot and fuming people stretched bumper to bumper for as far as he could see.

Cars from car factories.

Car factories that wouldn't exist if he hadn't invented them in the first place.

Mark looked at each exhaust pipe as it crawled past and at the fumes belching out. Black fumes, brown fumes, grey fumes, blue fumes, white fumes, see-through fumes.

He looked out over the rooftops and saw that the whole city was covered with a dirty smog haze.

I did that, he thought.

'Pino, more salami,' yelled Mrs Abrozetti from the front of the shop.

Pino didn't hear her.

He was sitting in the storeroom on a sack of

beans, holding a spoon out at arms length and staring at it.

He hoped it was the right type of spoon.

Smalley's book had just said a shiny spoon.

Pino had found the shiniest spoon in the whole shop, the one they used for the olives. It was stainless steel so it didn't pick up stains.

Hope the holes don't matter, he thought.

The holes were good for draining the olives but they might be a problem when you were trying to find out who you were in a past life.

You might find you were someone who'd been shot several times.

Pino's arm was aching.

He started moving the spoon towards his face, swinging it slowly from side to side.

Mrs Abrozetti appeared in the doorway.

'Hey,' she said angrily, 'this is a deli, not a beauty parlour. Lazy boy. Sometimes I think you're not an Abrozetti.'

The giant metal jaws ripped into the car and swung it high into the air. Glass showered down from the shattered windows.

Mark stood with his face pressed to the fence and watched as the crane dumped the flattened car onto a pile of other flattened cars.

The wrecker's yard was bigger than school and Dad's work and the supermarket carpark put together. It was full of piles of rusting car bodies.

Mark stood on tiptoe but he couldn't see where they ended.

Thousands of cars.

Millions probably.

I did that, he thought.

'You're not coming out of that pigsty till you clean it up,' shouted Mrs Wainwright outside Rufus's room.

Rufus didn't hear her.

He was lying on his bed, holding a spoon out at arms length and staring at it.

He wasn't sure why it had to be a spoon.

Smalley's book had said a spoon, but why not a fork or a knife?

That's the trouble with people who write books, thought Rufus, they think they know everything.

He started moving the spoon towards his face, slowly swinging it from side to side.

'I don't know where you get your filthy habits from,' shouted Mrs Wainwright outside the door. 'No wonder your father left home.'

Mark looked across the beach towards the oil refinery in the distance. He could see the sun glinting off the line of petrol tankers as they moved slowly past the storage tanks and the towers of the refinery itself.

Mark looked back down at the concrete pipe at his feet. Greeny-black liquid trickled out of the pipe and into the water, where it spread out into an ever-larger murky cloud.

I did that, thought Mark.

Mrs Abrozetti had given up calling Pino in the mornings. It was like trying to wake the dead. She'd found a better way than shouting herself hoarse.

Television.

As she did each morning, she switched it on and turned the sound up.

Pino opened his eyes. His bedroom door was open. Every night when he went to bed he closed it and every morning when he woke up it was open.

And the television was blaring.

He could see the screen from his bed. A fat man wearing leather shorts and braces was speaking German very slowly. Each time he said a word it appeared on the screen in print.

Every morning, thought Pino. If Mum wants me to learn German why doesn't she say so?

Then he remembered he'd just woken up and he was meant to be looking for clues.

On the screen the man was holding up a decorated beer mug.

'Ein Stein,' said the man.

Ein Stein said the words on the screen.

'Ein Stein,' said Pino.

His eyes widened.

Rufus always slept with his head under the pillow.

When Mum gave him his wake-up yell it made her sound as if she was in New Zealand.

It meant, though, that when he opened his eyes he couldn't see anything.

'Rufus,' yelled Mrs Wainwright, 'you're not going to school till you've cleaned up that pigsty.'

Rufus opened his eyes. He couldn't see anything. Then he remembered what he was meant to be looking for.

He slid his head out from under the pillow, eyes wide open.

The first thing he saw was red and flat.

His school folder.

Something was written on it.

'Wainwright'.

Rufus sat up, excitedly repeating the word to himself.

'Wainwright, Wainwright.'

Then his face fell.

'That's me.'

Daryl walked across the city square holding a spoon out in front of him and slowly swinging it from side to side.

This is dumb, he thought.

He'd been doing it for days, ever since he'd seen Mark doing it.

If Mark was going to turn out to have been a somebody in a past life, he was too. That's if he could get this dumb self-hypnosis to work.

Daryl stared at his reflection and swung the spoon faster. Suddenly he saw a flash of light and he was sitting on the ground and his head hurt.

He looked up at the stone column he'd just walked into. On top of it was a statue of a fierce-looking woman in a long dress.

Queen Victoria.

'Jeez,' said Daryl, 'I'm a woman.'

Pino and Rufus finally saw Mark sitting under a tree on the far side of the school oval. They ran over to him, shouting excitedly.

'Smalley! Smalley! It worked!'

'We know who we are!'

'I'm Albert Einstein,' yelled Pino, 'the greatest scientist who ever lived. I invented the theory of relatives.'

'I'm somebody Wainwright,' shouted Rufus. 'I don't know what he did yet but he's probably a relative of mine.'

'You're not the only one who's going to cream the project in,' said Pino as they reached Mark.

They stopped dead and stared.

Mark was tearing his Henry Ford project into little pieces.

11

Mark sat hunched in a cubicle in the school library video room and stared at the ancient black-and-white news film on the screen.

He watched himself, middle-aged and still wearing the funny-looking suit, walking around a car factory inspecting old-fashioned cars on the assembly line.

On the screen he looked very pleased with himself.

In the cubicle he wasn't pleased with himself at all.

I should have known, he thought. I should have known what inventing car factories would lead to.

Mark realized Annie was watching over his shoulder.

'I should have known,' he said.

'You should have,' she said. 'Couldn't you tell when you looked in the bathroom mirror how daggy that suit was?'

Mark glared at her.

'Sorry,' she said, 'I thought a joke might help.'

Mark sighed. He wished it could.

Annie sighed too.

'You're not the only one who should have known,' she said, and went back to her cubicle.

Mark followed.

'I've had to live with this for three months,' said Annie, 'ever since it was on television.'

She pressed the play button and old black-and-white film appeared on her screen.

It was a horse race. The Melbourne Cup, 1930. At first all Mark could see was a confusion of horses, all galloping like crazy. There were lots of shots of spectators getting excited, most of them looking as though they bought their clothes at the same shop as Henry Ford.

Then there was just Phar Lap, galloping to victory with great muscular strides.

Mark wished he'd looked that good in his past life.

He'd just started to wonder why Annie was looking so depressed when a reporter's voice started up on the video.

'Australia, they say, is in the grip of a gambling addiction,' said the reporter. The screen showed modern-day people queueing to place bets at a TAB. 'Experts believe,' continued the reporter, 'the habit often starts when a harmless once-a-year bet comes in a winner. By that reckoning, it seems safe to say that Phar Lap created more gambling addicts than any other Australian sporting champion.'

Annie stopped the tape.

'I should have known too,' she said. 'I wish I'd jumped the fence and run off to a paddock somewhere instead of winning all those Melbourne Cups.'

Mark looked at her distraught face and wished he

could say something to make her feel better. But all he could think of was that he wished he'd gone to the pictures instead of inventing the Model T Ford.

'Oh no!'

The shout had come from the next cubicle.

Mark and Annie peered in.

It was Pino, staring at a screen that was showing nuclear explosions and black-and-white cities with not a single building standing, and modern missiles being loaded into submarines.

'Without Einstein's principles of nuclear physics,' the voice-over was saying, 'there would have been no destruction of Hiroshima and Nagasaki, no arsenal of nuclear weapons for East and West to aim at each other.'

Pino stopped the tape.

They all looked at each other.

None of them knew what to say.

Rufus broke the silence, running in with a volume of an encyclopaedia.

'There's a Wainwright!' he said excitedly. 'Enoch Wainwright. I can't look. What do you think he'll be, a genius, a billionaire or a sporting legend?'

None of the others answered, so Rufus opened the encyclopaedia and read out loud.

'Enoch Wainwright. In 1593 he invented ... tarpaulin.' Rufus stared at the page. 'Tarpaulin?'

He looked at Mark, Annie and Pino, crushed.

'Well, this is a busy little group.'

It was Mr Cruickshank, smiling broadly.

'Wainwright and Abrozetti, doing research. Well done. Your new-found enthusiasm must be catching, Smalley. Keep it up. I'll be expecting something very special from all of you.'

Still smiling broadly, he went out.

Mark, Annie, Pino and Rufus looked at each other glumly.

At the end of the afternoon, as they walked out of school, they were still lost in their own gloomy thoughts.

It was Pino who broke the silence.

'Let's try and be positive,' he said. 'Forget about the bad stuff. There's heaps of good stuff to put in the project. What brand of toothpaste we used, stuff like that.'

'Where would the world be without tarpaulin?' said Rufus. 'No tents, nothing.'

'Let's do the project, get the best grades we can and stop being dags,' said Pino.

Mark was about to answer him when Daryl came running up waving a book about Queen Victoria.

'Mark! Mark!' he said, wide-eyed with alarm. 'This reckons I invaded Africa, India and China and killed thousands of people and took slaves and broke up families and made everyone read the Bible. I didn't, did I?'

Mark had always been proud of how he could be a solid big brother when he had to be. When Daryl's first tooth had come out early and Daryl had panicked and thought the Smurfs were taking him apart at night, it had been Mark who had put him at ease.

Now, though, Mark opened his mouth to say

something reassuring and nothing came out.

Pino grabbed the book and scanned the back cover.

'You weren't all bad,' he said to Daryl. 'As well as being Queen of England for most of the 1800s you were the greatest empress of modern times. You had hundreds of millions of subjects.'

But Daryl had seen the expression on Mark's face.

'There aren't hundreds of millions of subjects,' said Daryl glumly. 'There's only maths, English, geography . . .'

Mark put his hand on Daryl's shoulder.

'We're all in the same boat,' he said. 'We've all done crook things. I should have known what inventing car factories would lead to.'

'You should have known what feeding my hamster curried prawns would lead to,' said Rufus, 'but that didn't stop you.'

'I should have known what people betting on me would lead too,' said Annie to Daryl. 'When people get addicted to gambling, they'll gamble with anything, even the planet.'

'I'm not listening to any more of this,' said Pino, 'I'm getting on with the project. Did they have toothpaste early this century?'

'We can't ignore it,' said Mark. 'We did this stuff. We're responsible.'

'Easy for you,' said Pino. Suddenly he was on the verge of tears. 'You just invented a few car factories. I've brought the whole planet to the brink of nuclear destruction.'

Annie put her arm around him.

'You weren't to know,' she said.

'We've got to make up for what we've done,' said Mark.

There, he'd said it.

He'd been thinking it for hours but it had taken this long to actually say it.

The others stared at him.

'Oh, right, okay,' said Pino, 'I'll just pop over to America and Russia and tell them they can't use my principles of nuclear physics anymore.'

'I'm serious,' said Mark. 'We've got to make up for what we've done.'

'He's right,' said Annie.

'How?' said Daryl.

'How?' said Rufus.

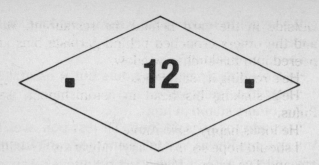

12

The proprietor of the Punjab Indian Restaurant hung the Closed sign on the door and walked slowly over to the till where his wife was massaging her feet and counting the night's takings.

'You go to bed, dear,' said the proprietor, 'I'll do the washing up.'

'Thanks, love,' said his wife with a tired smile.

The proprietor walked wearily towards the kitchen, mentally preparing himself for the mountain of curry-crusted pots, pans, plates and cutlery.

He pushed open the kitchen door and his jaw dropped.

Stacked neatly on the table were the pots, pans, plates and cutlery, all washed and dried and sparkling clean.

Pinned to the drying-up cloth was a note.

The proprietor picked it up and read it.

His jaw dropped even further.

'Sorry,' it said, signed 'Queen Victoria.'

Outside in the yard behind the restaurant, Mark and the others crouched behind garbage bins and peered into the kitchen window.

'He's reading it,' said Pino.

'He's shaking his head in astonishment,' said Rufus.

'He looks happy,' said Annie.

'I should hope so,' said Daryl. 'My arms are killing me and I've ripped Mum's rubber gloves. Fair go, I only invaded two continents.'

Mark watched as the proprietor smiled and scratched his head and sat down and read the note again.

'It's not much,' said Mark, 'but it's a start.'

The Japanese tourists stood in front of State Parliament House, smiling and chatting as they took photos of the building and each other and their tour leader.

Mark, Annie, Pino, Rufus and Daryl stood nearby, watching.

'Remember,' said Mark, 'relaxed and natural.'

Pino blew his cheeks out several times like he'd seen someone do once on World Championship Wrestling just before they went into the ring against The Detroit Killer.

'Straighten your hair,' said Rufus.

Pino ran his fingers through his hair.

'Good luck,' said Annie.

'Relaxed and natural,' said Mark.

Pino blew his cheeks out a few more times, then walked over to the Japanese tourists. Mark and the others followed a few paces behind.

'Greetings,' said Pino loudly. 'I come in peace.'

Mark and Annie swapped a pained look.

The tour leader looked at Pino with a puzzled expression.

'Hello,' she said, in Japanese.

'Look, er, it's like this,' said Pino. 'Ages and ages ago I came up with some principles of nuclear physics, and ... well, I didn't know they could be used for making bombs and things so I showed them to other people and they did and they ... dropped them on you.'

The tour leader and her party stared at Pino, brows wrinkled with incomprehension.

'World War Two,' said Pino. 'Bombs. Atom bombs. Nuclear.'

The Japanese tourists looked at each other and shrugged.

'Einstein,' said Pino.

The Japanese tourists repeated this to each other, mystified.

Pino realized he wasn't getting through. He made an explosion noise and threw his arms up in the air.

The tour leader's face lit up.

'Ah,' she said, 'fireworks. Very pretty.'

'Hiroshima,' said Pino desperately. 'Nagasaki.'

The Japanese tourists looked suddenly grave and murmured among themselves.

'Please,' said the tour leader, putting her hand on Pino's arm. 'You too young. Not your fault.'

'No, it was, it was, and I want to make it up to you,' said Pino.

The tour leader was looking mystified again.

Pino decided to try using shorter sentences.

'Make,' he said. 'It. Up. To. You.'

The tour leader still didn't understand.

Mark stepped forward.

'We'd like you to come with us,' he said. 'Please.'

Once Mark and Annie and Pino and Rufus and Daryl had persuaded the tour leader to climb through the hole in the fence, the rest of her party followed.

Annie saw a couple of the Japanese tourists throwing nervous glances back at their tour bus parked at the kerb.

'It's okay,' she said, 'it's Sunday. No parking cops on Sunday.'

Mark led them across the demolition site, thankful that Dad and his mates weren't doing weekend overtime.

He stopped by a half-demolished old building, picked up a sledgehammer and handed it to Pino.

Pino waited till the Japanese tourists had gathered round, then swung the sledgehammer into the wall, knocking out a couple of bricks.

The Japanese tourists looked at each other, mystified.

Mark took the sledgehammer from Pino and handed it to the burliest of the male tourists.

'Hiroshima, Nagasaki,' said Pino. 'Now it's your turn.'

The burly Japanese tourist looked puzzled. He glanced at the tour leader. She looked puzzled too.

Pino and Mark mimed swinging the hammer into the wall.

The burly Japanese tourist swung the hammer into the wall. Part of it collapsed.

The other Japanese tourists applauded.

The burly Japanese tourist grinned.

He swung the hammer again and another piece of wall fell down.

The others applauded loudly.

And suddenly they all wanted a go. Mark, Annie, Pino, Rufus and Daryl gathered up all the hammers and picks they could find and pressed them into eager hands.

Rufus handed a pick to an elderly man.

'Have you ever had any major disasters in Japan involving tarpaulin?' he asked hopefully.

The man looked blank. 'Tar-pau-rin?' he said.

'Doesn't matter,' said Rufus sadly.

Soon the demolition site was ringing with excited shouts and the crash of falling bricks.

Pino, beaming, appeared through the clouds of dust and gave Mark a punch on the arm.

'Great, eh?' said Pino.

'Yeah,' said Mark.

It's still only a start though, he thought.

13

Mark and Annie stood on the front doorstep of a small suburban cottage.

Annie rang the bell.

'Do you speak any Russian?' asked Mark.

'Mrs Karpovsky speaks English,' said Annie. 'She used to clean our house before the Berlin Wall came down.'

'Why did she stop?' asked Mark.

'Dad reckoned Russians weren't persecuted anymore, so he hired a single mother.'

The door opened and a plump elderly woman saw Annie and beamed.

'They're American,' said Mark.

'Are you sure?' said Pino.

'She's got Texas written on her cap,' said Mark. 'Come on.'

He and Pino went over to the American couple photographing the art gallery.

'Excuse me,' said Mark, 'would you like some soup from the Russian people?'

The Americans stared at him.

'What say?' said the man. 'Soup?'

Mark and Pino pointed to where Mrs Karpovsky, Annie, Rufus and Daryl were standing with the refreshment trolley that Pino's dad hired out for weddings. A steaming metal tub stood on the trolley, and a sign saying 'The Russian People Greet The American People – Free Soup.'

'It's their way of saying g'day ... I mean hi,' said Pino. 'And not to worry about all the nuclear weapons.'

'Russian soup?' said the woman, intrigued.

Mark and Pino led the couple over to the trolley, where Mrs Karpovsky gave them a winning smile.

'The Russians are great people,' said Annie to the couple. 'Reliable, generous, kind to animals. They're always giving people soup.'

'And tarpaulin,' said Rufus.

Mrs Karpovsky ladled out two bowls of steaming beetroot soup and handed them to the Americans.

'Very pleased to meet you,' she said in her thick accent. 'You have a wonderful country. I love *Dallas*.'

The Americans broke into broad grins.

'Heck, we're from Dallas and we thank you kindly,' said the man.

'Where are you from?' asked the woman.

'Woodville,' said Mrs Karpovsky.

'Really?' said the woman. 'Is that near Moscow?'

Mark watched the Americans chatting happily with Mrs Karpovsky and drinking the soup.

Still only a start, he thought.

Then Mark had the idea of making the signs and that's when things started to go wrong.

The first sign said 'Detour'.

They used the biggest piece of wood from the pile at the side of Mark's house, and some yellow paint left over from when Bob had touched up the rust on the Falcon.

They carried the sign to Waratah Park, which gave them all blisters on their hands.

Mark chose Waratah Park because so much traffic used the road through the park as a short cut to avoid the Edgar Street intersection.

He went over to a tree growing right on the edge of the road.

'I know this isn't much,' he said to the tree, 'not from the bloke who's responsible for all the car fumes you have to put up with, but it's all I can manage at the moment. Enjoy your day off.'

He patted the trunk, then went back to the others and helped them prop the Detour sign up in the middle of the road.

The first three vehicles, all cars, slowed down and turned up the side street that led away from the park.

The next vehicle, a semi-trailer carrying bags of cement, didn't.

It drove straight over the sign and smashed it to pieces.

The next sign they made said 'Sorry' with a large arrow at the bottom.

They used the second-largest piece of wood from the pile at the side of the house and some corrosion-resistant lilac paint left over from when Annie's mum had painted the card-table on the boat.

They wheeled the sign to the car wrecker's yard on Daryl's skateboard, which left one of the wheels wobbly.

'Daryl,' said Mark gently, 'what's more important? A skateboard or saying sorry to the people who have to walk past this every day?'

He pointed to the piles of rusting cars.

'Yeah,' said Daryl indignantly, 'well, there's probably a place like this somewhere with piles of rusting skateboards, and that's where mine's going to end up now, isn't it?'

'We'll fix it,' said Annie.

'You can have my skateboard,' said Pino.

'I don't think a monarch should be riding a skateboard in the first place,' said Rufus.

They wired the Sorry sign to the wrecker's yard fence with the arrow pointing to the piles of car bodies and waited for someone to walk past so they could explain what it meant.

Before anyone did, the wrecker came and made them take it down.

'We're not having a go at you,' said Mark. 'I'm the one who's to blame.'

'What are you,' said the wrecker, 'loony or Candid Camera?'

Nobody made them take the sign down from next to the oil refinery waste pipe at the beach.

Mostly because in four hours nobody saw it but them.

'This is ridiculous,' said Pino.

'We could be here for weeks,' said Rufus.

'My skateboard's leaving now,' said Daryl.

'It does seem a waste of time,' said Annie, 'if no one's going to see it here.'

'You're right,' said Mark.

They loaded the sign back onto the skateboard.

The sign wasn't any more successful when they put it in Mark's front yard with the arrow pointing to the dead saplings.

A few people walked past, but they ignored the Sorry sign just like they'd been ignoring the FOR SALE sign for the past three years.

Mark and the others sat leaning against the house and stared gloomily at the sign nobody wanted to see.

'Told you we should have made a larger sign,' said Rufus. 'Big bit of tarpaulin.'

'Rufus,' said Annie wearily.

'We're not reaching enough people,' said Mark. 'We need something people can't ignore.'

'Mum and Dad won't ignore it when they get back from the shops,' said Daryl.

Mark turned and looked at Annie and saw she had the same expression on her face as the morning of the excursion when her mum had driven off.

'Maybe we're trying to do too much,' she said softly.

'What about our projects?' said Pino. 'We could use them. People don't ignore them. Everyone reads my projects at our place. Even Gran, and she can't even speak English.'

'That's it,' said Annie, brightening. 'We'll make our projects letters of apology.'

'We could make copies and stick them in people's mail boxes,' said Rufus.

'Yes,' said Annie and Pino.

Rufus, surprised, beamed happily.

Mark listened to them and suddenly felt heavy inside and tired all over.

He knew what they were planning wasn't enough, and yet what else could they do?

Annie turned to him and saw his gloomy expression.

She squeezed his arm.

'We're only kids,' she said.

14

Mark gave it a go.

'Dear People Of The World,' he wrote. 'Sorry.'

Then he stopped.

Next to him at the library table, Annie, Pino and Rufus wrote on, filling line after line.

Mark couldn't.

What's the point, he thought. What's the point of apologizing if you can't make things better?

A voice cut into his thoughts.

'Nice of you all to drop in.'

Mr Cruickshank was striding grimly towards them across the library.

'I've just been explaining to my colleagues,' continued Mr Cruickshank, 'why none of you have been at school for three days. Working on their projects, I said. Better be good projects, they said. They will be, I said.'

There was a silence while Mark and the others looked at Mr Cruickshank and Mr Cruickshank looked at them.

'May I see what you've written so far?' said Mr Cruickshank.

Slowly, one by one, they held up their folders.

Annie was on her second page.

Pino had nearly finished his first.

Rufus had done more than half a page.

Mr Cruickshank glanced at the pages without reading them.

Then he glanced at Mark's line and a half.

He looked at Mark for a long time.

'This is less than you had a week ago, Smalley,' he said eventually.

'I've had some different ideas, sir,' said Mark.

Mr Cruickshank's voice took on a tone Mark had never heard before.

'I hope they're good ones, Smalley, because if they're not I'm going to have to agree with what some of my colleagues are saying. That you'd be better off in a different school.'

Mark stared at him.

Annie grabbed the folders and thrust them at Mr Cruickshank.

'Please sir,' she said, 'read these and you'll understand.'

Mr Cruickshank opened his mouth to say something.

'Please sir,' she said.

With a long-suffering sigh Mr Cruickshank took the folders and read what they'd written.

'Not bad,' he said. 'I wouldn't have called Phar Lap a famous person from history, but I suppose I can allow it. The apology approach is a nice idea. Shame which ever one of you had it let the others pinch it.'

'Sir,' said Mark, 'you don't understand.'

'I understand,' said Mr Cruickshank, holding up Mark's folder, 'that nothing I've read here excuses this appalling slackness by you.'

'But it's all true,' said Annie. 'I'm Phar Lap. Mark's Henry Ford. Pino's Albert Einstein. Rufus is Enoch Wainwright. We're responsible.'

Mr Cruickshank looked at Annie.

'Upton,' he said, 'don't be silly.'

He turned and walked out of the library.

Mark looked at the others.

'We've got to accept it,' he said. 'They won't listen.'

Walking home from the bus stop, Mark remembered what Annie had said.

'We're only kids.'

He realized what she'd meant.

She hadn't meant they were only kids.

She'd meant the world thought they were only kids.

Which was why nobody would listen to them.

Mark suddenly wished he still had his Henry Ford body, wrinkled skin and moustache and funny-looking suit and all. Then, when he said he was sorry and explained to the world the mistakes he'd made, they'd listen and understand and help him put things right.

But his Henry Ford body was a pile of dust in the ground somewhere, or a jar of ashes on a mantlepiece.

A memory, thought Mark gloomily, like the Mark

Smalley who was once Dux of the School. All that was left was the Mark Smalley who got Ds, and nobody had any faith in him at all.

Bob lay under the Falcon and glared.

Twenty minutes he'd been trying to loosen the exhaust bracket and all he'd loosened was some skin on his knuckles.

He tightened the wrench and tried again.

No good.

Bloody car, he thought. Whoever invented this bloody thing should be strung up.

He started bashing the bracket with the wrench.

Then he stopped.

Because he wasn't angry with the car, or the person who invented it.

He was angry with himself.

And confused and sad and frightened.

All because of what he'd just found in Mark's room.

Mark walked gloomily in through the front gate and Bob slid out from under the Falcon.

Mark saw the serious expression on Bob's face.

He's been having trouble getting that exhaust off, thought Mark.

'G'day, champ,' said Bob. 'Daryl's at a mate's and Mum's at her gardening class. So we can have a little chat.'

Mark knew they wouldn't be chatting about the exhaust.

The project was on the kitchen table.

As Mark stared at it, all he could see was the big red D and all he could hear was a siren going past outside.

He didn't care anymore.

Bob cleared his throat.

'I've been thinking,' he said, 'about why you didn't show this to me . . . and I reckon I sort of know.'

Mark started to protest that he'd tried to, then thought, why bother.

'Let me finish, mate,' said Bob.

Mark watched him walk slowly around the kitchen, and waited for the disappointment to seep into his weather-beaten face.

It didn't.

Instead Bob came over to Mark and stood in front of him.

'I've been putting a lot of pressure on you,' he said softly, 'too much pressure, I reckon, 'cause I was worried you didn't know what was important, like I didn't know what was important when I was your age.'

Mark felt his heart start to beat faster.

Bob picked up the project from the table.

'I've been thinking a bit since I found this . . . and I reckon if you're the smart kid I'm always saying you are, then you do know what's important.'

Mark's heart was pounding in his chest.

'I'm going to keep off your back from now on,' said Bob, ''cause I know that whatever you do, it'll be your best.'

A truck roared past outside.

Bob thought of the quiet leafy street Mark would live in one day when he was a somebody.

'And I know,' he said, 'you've got the guts and the ability to finish what you've started.'

Bob looked at Mark to see if Mark felt that way and saw from the determination shining in Mark's eyes that he did.

Annie, Pino, Rufus and Daryl stared at Mark in amazement.

'You're out of your brain,' said Rufus.

'You're joking,' said Pino.

'I don't think he is,' said Annie.

Mark went over to Annie's window and looked out at the city skyline.

'If we're serious about making people listen,' he said, 'we'll do a project they can't ignore. That means telly.'

'How are we going to get on telly?' said Pino.

Mark turned to them.

'We'll get on the news,' he said.

'How?' said Annie.

'Mark could do the drying up,' muttered Daryl.

'We'll make some news,' said Mark.

The others were still staring at him, but now they were fascinated.

'Make some news?' said Annie.

Mark looked around the walls at the Phar Lap posters and cuttings.

'With Phar Lap's help,' he said.

15

The museum attendant switched off the last of the lights and the museum was in darkness.

'Night, Des,' called a colleague on his way out to the carpark.

'Night, Phil,' called back the attendant.

He shone his torch onto a large Egyptian mummy lying in a glass case.

'Night, Gavin,' said the attendant.

The mummy didn't reply, but then the attendant hadn't expected it to.

Underneath the display case next to Gavin's, Mark and Annie huddled down as small as they could and prayed for the attendant to go.

He went.

They heard him open the door to the carpark, step out, and close it behind him.

Mark switched his torch on and looked at his watch.

Right on time.

'Okay,' he said, 'ten minutes to be sure.'

He switched off the torch.

They waited.

As Mark's eyes slowly got used to the darkness, he became aware of the dark shape of the mummy in the case above them.

A body, thousands of years old.

All that trouble those ancient Egyptians took to preserve the body of a king, he thought, and there was no need because the king's probably alive and well and at this very moment working in a take-away restaurant.

'Ten minutes is up,' whispered Annie.

They crawled out from under the case and stretched their cramped legs.

Then they moved slowly and carefully to the door, keeping their torch beams low.

At the door they shone the torches onto the alarm box.

'You're sure it's the same?' said Mark anxiously.

'Yes,' said Annie. 'The people at the yacht club are always losing the key to theirs, so they've discovered that if you do this . . .'

She switched it off and on several times, very fast.

Mark held his breath.

'. . . you can turn it off without a key.'

She turned the alarm off and opened the door to the carpark.

Mark flashed his torch three times and saw a torch flashed three times in reply.

Then he heard a rattling and clattering as the others approached with the trolleys.

They'd done a good job. Four matching super-market trolleys, two in front and two behind, wired together with old coat-hangers.

'Not a bung wheel on any of 'em,' said Pino proudly.

'Unlike my skateboard,' said Daryl.

'Give it a rest,' said Rufus.

They steered the trolleys through the dark museum and into the National Treasures Exhibition.

Mark went in first, and there, in the torchlight, was a grim, black-bearded face staring at him.

Mark leapt back and collided with the trolleys and then saw the plough that could jump over tree-stumps. He looked back at the bearded face and saw that it was flat.

'It's a painting, Smalley,' said Pino, rolling his eyes. 'You'll be panicking at your own shadow next.'

'Boo,' said Rufus, stepping out from behind the door.

Pino jumped and dropped his torch.

'Come on, you lot,' said Daryl. 'Stop mucking around and let's get the horse into the trolleys.'

'Just a sec,' said Mark.

Annie had found Phar Lap.

As she moved towards it, torch held out, the big horse seemed to loom majestically out of the darkness, glass eyes glinting.

Annie gently ran her hand along Phar Lap's flank.

'Sorry about this, body,' she said, 'but I need you back for a bit.'

Then she signalled to the others and they wheeled the trolleys over.

Lifting Phar Lap up high enough to lower him into the supermarket trolleys took all their strength. At last he was safely in, one leg in each trolley. They caught their breath, panting and sweating.

'Okay,' said Mark, 'let's go.'

They wheeled Phar Lap through the museum and into the carpark, closing the door behind them.

Now they were outside, the moonlight gleamed on Phar Lap's coat.

'The tarpaulin,' said Rufus.

They dragged Bob's picnic tarpaulin out of one of the trolleys and unrolled it and pulled it over Phar Lap so that none of him was visible.

Then they set off for the phone box.

It was in a street that ran off the side-street next to the museum.

They parked Phar Lap in the shadow of a tree, and Mark went into the phone box.

He dialled the number written on his hand.

It answered.

'Hello?' he said, 'Is that the TV news-room?'

The person at the other end said yes.

'I've got some big news for you,' said Mark. 'Phar Lap's just been kidnapped. He'll be giving a press conference in thirty minutes at the casino.'

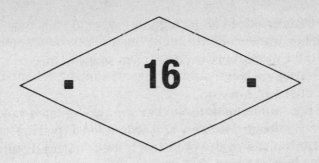

16

'**D**on't slow down,' said Mark.

Now that there were only three of them to do the pushing, the going was harder.

They were clattering along a back street that ran parallel with the main street the museum was in, and the road surface was full of cracks and potholes.

'Phar Lap coming up on the outside in the Supermarket Trolley Handicap,' said Daryl in his best racecaller's voice.

Mark could see that Annie wasn't amused.

'Daryl,' he said, 'shut up.'

Daryl muttered something.

Mark ignored him.

He had other things to worry about.

Like whether Pino and Rufus were going okay.

Pino and Rufus pounded on Mr Cruickshank's front door until Mr Cruickshank opened it and stood staring at them in surprise.

'Abrozetti, Wainwright, what are you doing here?'

'You've got to come with us, sir,' said Pino. 'We're doing our project.'

Mr Cruickshank tried to make sense of this.

'Your project?'

'Yes sir. Hurry up.'

Mr Cruickshank looked at the two agitated boys on his front doorstep and wondered if picking up litter on the oval would teach them not to disturb teachers at home.

'See me in the morning if you want to talk about your project. Now go away.'

He sighed and started to close the door.

'We want you to see our project tonight, sir, in person, sir,' said Rufus. 'In case the TV news leaves bits out.'

Mr Cruickshank opened the door and stared at them in alarm.

'TV news?'

The museum attendant strode through the dark museum, torchlight flashing around him, calling himself a number of words he wouldn't usually have used in front of the exhibits.

He'd been halfway home, looking forward to giving his wife her birthday present, when he'd remembered he'd left it in his locker.

'Forget my own head if it wasn't prominently displayed,' he muttered.

He strode on, torchlight flashing over an empty platform with four hoof-marks on it.

He took three more strides, then stopped and turned and shone his torch all over the platform.

The empty platform.

He shone his torch all around the room.

Even up on the ceiling.

Then he ran for the phone.

Mark heard the police sirens just as he thought his legs were going to seize up.

He and Annie and Daryl dragged the trollies to a halt and looked round, trying to work out where the sirens were coming from.

The museum.

Then Mark saw a girl and a boy leaning against a wall on the other side of the street locked in a kiss.

The girl, looking over her boyfriend's shoulder, was staring at them and making loud moaning noises.

Mark realized why.

When they'd stopped suddenly the tarpaulin had slipped down and Phar Lap's head was poking out.

They dragged the tarpaulin back in place.

Mark heard the young man, whose back was to them and who thought his girlfriend was making noises of approval rather than alarm, make some of his own.

'Mmm mmmmm mmmmmmmm.'

Mark and Annie and Daryl threw themselves at the trollies and rattled and clattered off towards the casino.

Soon the moans were left behind and all they could hear were sirens.

Mark realized his legs weren't hurting anymore.

It was a quiet night in the television news-room.

The journalist wandered out of the viewing room where she'd been looking at some stand-by dog stories.

'Thin night,' she said to the new cadet on phone duty. 'Might have to use a fido.'

The cadet looked at his shorthand pad.

'All I've got's some racehorse owner's been kid-napped,' he said. 'Asian I think.'

'What's his name?' said the journalist with a bored yawn.

The cadet struggled to read his shorthand.

'Har Lap.'

No, that wasn't right.

'Far Lap.'

The journalist stared at him, then dived for the phone.

This was the tricky bit.

Crossing the main road to get into the under-ground carpark.

Once they were in there they could go under-ground all the rest of the way to the casino, safe from the police cars.

Mark peered round the corner and down the street towards the museum.

The museum was surrounded by flashing blue lights.

The sirens were deafening now.

Jammed traffic was building up. Soon the road in front of them would be blocked and they'd never get across.

'Come on,' said Mark.

'They'll see us,' said Daryl. 'I bet you four litres of strawberry ripple they see us.'

'Isn't there any other way we can go?' said Annie.

Mark shook his head.

Then they heard it.

The police helicopter.

It was over the museum, beaming its spotlight down onto the surrounding streets.

It was heading in their direction.

'Come on,' yelled Mark.

There was a break in the traffic and they hurled the trolleys into it, feet pounding on the tarmac, trolley-wheels screeching, vibrations from the trolleys stinging their hands.

They hit the opposite kerb with a thump that had Phar Lap rearing up so high Mark thought they were a goner but the four legs clanged back down into the trolleys and they clattered down the ramp into the underground carpark.

Safe.

For now.

'He's been like it for several days,' said Joy, wiping the suds off her hands.

Bob stopped trying to watch the news.

'Like what, exactly?' he said.

'I don't know,' said Joy. 'Sort of tense and secretive. Ever since you had that chat with him about that D he got.'

Bob frowned. That chat was meant to make Mark feel relaxed, not tense.

'Where did you say they both are?' he asked.

'Daryl's at Nick Chen's and Mark's at Pino Abrozetti's,' said Joy. 'Mark said he was working with Pino on the project and Daryl said something about Queen Victoria.'

'Daryl's not studying Queen Victoria, is he?' said Bob, puzzled.

'I don't know,' said Joy. 'And Bob, there's something else. Mark said he was working with Pino on the project, but he didn't take this.'

She held out Mark's folder.

Bob took it, heart sinking.

A one-off D was one thing. Mark going off with Pino when he was meant to be working was another.

Let's see just how far he's got with this project, thought Bob.

He opened the folder.

And found himself looking at a hand-drawn map. It showed a route from the museum to the casino. In the museum was an X and next to it was written Phar Lap. A dotted line ran from the X to the casino.

Bob stared at the map.

In his day if you'd handed in a crummy hand-drawn map for a piece of schoolwork you'd have got a belting. Nowdays it could be part of a new-fangled, prize-winning project.

Then Joy grabbed his arm and pointed to the television.

'In a report just to hand,' the newsreader was saying, 'Phar Lap, on loan to the Australian National Treasures Exhibition, has been taken out of the museum building . . .'

Bob and Joy stared at scenes of police searching the museum grounds by floodlight.

Then at a reporter standing outside the casino.

'An anonymous phone tip-off,' said the reporter, 'claimed that Phar Lap would be arriving here at any minute. So far, no sign of the legendary horse ...'

Bob leapt to his feet.

'Stay by the phone, love,' he said.

He ran out to the car with a lead weight growing in his chest.

17

Mark crept up the exit ramp of the underground carpark and peeked out at the casino.

Chaos.

Traffic was banked up as far as he could see, horns blowing and angry heads poking out of car windows.

At the casino entrance a crowd was milling around, shoving and shouting. Mark could see casino door-men and people in evening dress and people in ordinary clothes and people with TV cameras and police trying to get everyone to shut up.

He could hear the police helicopter almost overhead.

No way they'd get in that way.

He ran back down the ramp to the others.

'Back way,' he said, and they wheeled Phar Lap between the parked cars to the service lift.

It was slow going, just as it had been all the way through the carpark, because Phar Lap's head almost brushed the roof and they had to make sure they didn't brain him on the sprinklers.

They reached the lift and Mark pressed the Up button.

'Do they still hang people for stealing horses?' asked Daryl.

'Don't worry,' said Annie, 'we've got my permission.'

The lift doors opened and they wheeled Phar Lap in.

'Got the press release?' said Annie as they went up.

Mark nodded.

'Got the emergency stuff?' he said.

Annie pulled a plastic cylinder from her pocket and gave it to him.

Nautical Flare, it said, For Emergency Use Only.

Mark stuffed it into his pocket.

'Let's hope we don't need it,' he said.

He tried to sound more at ease than he felt. He hadn't actually been up in the lift when he'd checked out the route, and he wasn't sure what they'd find when the lift doors opened.

The lift doors opened and they wheeled Phar Lap out into a long corridor.

From the clattering of plates and banging of utensils, Mark guessed the corridor ran past the casino kitchens.

'Okay,' he said, 'we don't stop for anything.'

'Can I go to the toilet first?' asked Daryl.

'No,' said Mark.

They clattered down the corridor, the walls blurring past.

Mark glimpsed the startled faces of a couple of

men in white hats, but nothing got in their way until they reached the door at the end of the corridor.

Mark took a deep breath, flung the door open and they clattered through.

Chaos.

People milling around, falling over themselves to get out of the way of the advancing trolleys.

Mark realized they were in the casino foyer, and that the crowd from outside had come spilling in.

'Keep going,' he yelled to Annie and Daryl.

He could see a pair of big wooden doors on the other side of the foyer.

'Aim for the doors,' he shouted, 'that must be the casino.'

Suddenly other hands were grabbing the trolley handles and for a moment Mark thought people were trying to drag Phar Lap away.

Then he saw it was Pino and Rufus.

'Cruickshank's here,' said Pino, 'but we've lost him.'

'Tarpaulin,' yelled Rufus, 'where's the tarpaulin?'

Mark realized it had fallen off.

'We don't need it,' he shouted. 'We're here.'

With a crash they hit the doors and burst through.

In the huge chandelier-hung gaming room, startled faces turned from the card tables and roulette wheels and spinning two-up coins to gape at the huge auburn-coloured horse clattering into the room, fire from the chandeliers reflecting in its angry eyes.

Mark and the others dragged the trolleys to a halt.

They looked around at the hundreds of faces staring at them.

Reporters and TV cameras had followed them in and were jostling for position.

A roulette ball tinkled to a stop.

Silence.

Mark pulled the press release from his pocket, unfolded it and started reading in the loudest voice he could.

'Thank you for coming,' he said. 'I have here a press release issued tonight by Phar Lap, Henry Ford, Albert Einstein, Enoch Wainwright and Queen Victoria.'

He glanced at Annie, Pino, Rufus and Daryl and saw the proud and determined expressions on their faces.

Suddenly Annie pointed to the back of the crowd.

'Mr Cruickshank!' she shouted. 'Mr Cruickshank! Could you let Mr Cruickshank through, he's our teacher.'

The crowd parted.

Mr Cruickshank looked behind him, trying to pretend he wasn't Mr Cruickshank.

Everyone was looking at him.

He felt his face turning beetroot and his knees turning to jelly. He wished he was a mining executive like his father so he could make a hole appear in the floor and disappear into it.

Mark carried on with the press release and all eyes turned back to him.

'We're here to say sorry,' he said, 'but before we do, we want to say something else. Men and women of Australia, we're gambling with more than the housekeeping. We're gambling with the planet . . .'

Mark realized there was movement in the crowd.

Dinner-suited attendants and uniformed police-men were pushing towards him.

'They're not listening!' yelled Annie. 'Run for it!'

Darting into the crowd, weaving and twisting past startled bodies, they ran for it.

18

Bob saw the traffic jam ahead and braked and thumped the steering wheel in frustration.

Further up ahead he could see blue lights flashing and hear sirens wailing.

Cop cars?

Ambulances?

All those times the cops down the pub had joked about shooting first and asking questions later.

And he'd laughed.

Now Bob found himself staring at the Saint Christopher medal stuck to the dashboard.

Please, Mate, he thought, please don't let Mark or Daryl get hurt. Nothing else is important. The house, their careers, nothing. Just don't let them die.

He got out of the car and ran towards the casino.

Mark burst through the crush of bodies at the casino entrance.

Cars.

Cars everywhere.

He could hear shouts from the attendants and police further back in the confusion of bodies.

He saw Annie looking round wildly next to him and Pino next to her. Rufus and Daryl clawed their way out of the crowd.

They tried to press forward but there were too many cars.

The road was jammed.

People staring at them out of car windows.

Even the footpath was blocked.

Police cars, doors open and blue lights flashing.

Mark saw two uniformed figures scrambling out of one, pointing and shouting.

Annie grabbed him and yelled in his ear.

'Emergency plan!'

It was all they had left.

Mark jumped up onto the bonnet of the nearest car and pulled the flare from his pocket.

Okay, Mr Cruickshank, he thought, it worked for you, let's hope it works for us.

He grabbed the striking plate and scraped it over the live end.

Red sparks hissed out.

Mark held the cylinder above his head as a blinding red flame erupted from it.

The crowd at his feet froze.

Reporters, camera crews, police, attendants, doormen, casino patrons and other onlookers stared up at the flame and the boy holding it.

Good on you, Shanksie, thought Mark.

He looked down at the faces. The cameras. The microphones.

Now or never.

'Me and my friends'll be arrested in a minute,' yelled Mark, 'and go to court and all that stuff. We're not going till we've said this.'

'That's right,' yelled Pino.

Mark saw Pino and Rufus and Annie and Daryl, standing at his feet facing the crowd defiantly.

He didn't see Bob, standing in the crowd to one side, staring at him and Daryl in stunned horror.

'We came here to apologize,' yelled Mark, 'me and Albert and Enoch and Victoria and Phar. And we are sorry. But we also think it's not fair. We think it's not fair that when we were stuffing the planet up we were heroes and now we want to fix it up we're just kids.'

Bob looked around at the journalists and TV people and police and casino officials and expensively dressed punters hanging on every word being yelled by his son.

'Saying sorry,' said Mark, 'is the first part of our project. It's just the beginning of it. It's going to be a long project. We don't know when it'll finish. Our teacher, Mr Cruickshank, probably won't be around to mark it.'

Bob stared.

This?

The project?

Mark still hadn't seen him.

'My Dad's always going on about being successful,' said Mark, 'and he's right.'

Next to Bob the door of a big BMW opened and a man in a dinner suit looked out.

'I'll shift that kid,' growled the man, climbing out.

'Let him speak,' said Bob, pushing him back down.

'When we've been arrested and punished and all that's over,' said Mark, 'we're going to spend the rest of our lives trying to make a success of it. The planet.'

'That's right,' yelled Annie.

'Yeah,' yelled Daryl and Pino.

'Tarpaulin yes, plastic no,' yelled Rufus.

Then Mark saw Bob, leaning against the door of a large BMW with a red-faced man inside it.

He didn't have time to look at Bob for long because he could feel the flare getting hot as it got close to burning out and he could see the police starting to move forward.

'We dunno how we'll solve all the problems yet,' Mark said, 'but we'll think of something. What we've learnt from history is you can't wait for somebody else to do it. There isn't a somebody else. We're the somebodies.'

He looked back down at Bob.

He saw the way Bob was looking at him.

It wasn't the way Bob had looked at him at the primary school prize-giving.

It was puzzled and thoughtful rather than proud and contented.

But Mark's eyes were shining as he turned back to meet Annie and Pino and Rufus and Daryl's gaze and give one last triumphant urgent shout as the police moved in.

'We're the somebodies.'

Bumface

by

Morris Gleitzman

Bumface! That's who Angus wants to be. He dreams of being bold, brave, wild and free. Like the pirate in the stories he tells his younger brother and sister.

Instead Angus is just plain tired from changing nappies and wiping food off walls.

His mum calls him Mr Dependable, which is bad enough. Another baby would be a disaster. So Angus comes up with a bold and brave plan to stop her getting pregnant.

READ MORE IN PUFFIN

For children of all ages, Puffin represents quality and variety – the very best in publishing today around the world.

For complete information about books available from Puffin – and Penguin – and how to order them, contact us at the appropriate address below. Please note that for copyright reasons the selection of books varies from country to country.

On the worldwide web: www.penguin.co.uk

In the United Kingdom: Please write to *Dept. EP, Penguin Books Ltd, Bath Road, Harmondsworth, West Drayton, Middlesex UB7 ODA*

In the United States: Please write to *Penguin Putnam inc., P.O. Box 12289, Dept B, Newark, New Jersey 07101-5289* or call 1-800-788-6262

In Canada: Please write to *Penguin Books Canada Ltd, 10 Alcorn Avenue, Suite 300, Toronto, Ontario M4V 3B2*

In Australia: Please write to *Penguin Books Australia Ltd, P.O. Box 257, Ringwood, Victoria 3134*

In New Zealand: Please write to *Penguin Books (NZ) Ltd, Private Bag 102902, North Shore Mail Centre, Auckland 10*

In India: Please write to *Penguin Books India Pvt Ltd, 11 Panscheel Shopping Centre, Panscheel Park, New Delhi 110 017*

In the Netherlands: Please write to *Penguin Books Netherlands bv, Postbus 3507, NL-1001 AH Amsterdam*

In Germany: Please write to *Penguin Books Deutschland GmbH, Metzlerstrasse 26, 60594 Frankfurt am Main*

In Spain: Please write to *Penguin Books S. A., Bravo Murillo 19, 1° B, 28015 Madrid*

In Italy: Please write to *Penguin Italia s.r.l., Via Felice Casati 20, I–20124 Milano*

In France: Please write to *Penguin France S. A., 17 rue Lejeune, F–31000 Toulouse*

In Japan: Please write to *Penguin Books Japan, Ishikiribashi Building, 2–5–4, Suido, Bunkyo-ku, Tokyo 112*

In South Africa: Please write to *Longman Penguin Southern Africa (Pty) Ltd, Private Bag X08, Bertsham 2013*